TOLD UNDER
THE CITY UMBRELLA

Selected by the Literature Committee
of the Association for
Childhood Education International

Illustrated by Lisl Weil

MACMILLAN PUBLISHING CO., INC.
New York

Macmillan Publishing Co., Inc.
866 Third Avenue, New York, N.Y. 10022
Collier-Macmillan Canada Ltd.

Library of Congress catalog card number: 72–165107

Printed in the United States of America

10 9 8 7 6 5 4 3 2

ACKNOWLEDGMENTS

The Literature Committee of the Association for Childhood Education
International is grateful to the following publishers for permission to
reprint excerpts from the works listed below:

Atheneum Publishers—from *The Spider Plant* by Yetta Speevack,
Copyright © 1965 by Yetta Speevack; from A *Trainful of Strangers* by
Eleanor Hull, Copyright © 1968 by Eleanor Hull.

Coward-McCann, Inc.—from *The Street of the Flower Boxes* by
Peggy Mann, Copyright © 1966 by Peggy Mann; from *Who's in Charge
of Lincoln* by Dale Fife, illustrated by Paul Galdone, text Copyright ©
1965 by Dale Fife.

Farrar, Straus & Giroux, Inc.—from *The Cricket in Times Square* by
George Selden, illustrated by Garth Williams, copyright © 1960 by
George Selden Thompson and Garth Williams.

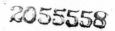

FOREWORD

Told Under the City Umbrella is the eighth and newest member of the "Umbrella" series for children, which includes *Told Under the Green Umbrella* (folk and fairy stories), *Told Under the Blue Umbrella* (stories "real and nearly real"), *Sung Under the Silver Umbrella* (poetry), *Told Under the Magic Umbrella* (modern fanciful tales), *Told Under Spacious Skies* (regional stories about American children), *Told Under the Stars and Stripes* (stories of varied ethnic groups in America), and *Told Under the Christmas Tree* (Christmas stories and poems), all published by The Macmillan Company, with selections made by various Literature Committees serving the Association for Childhood Education International.

The present Committee, working over a two-year period to select stories for this volume, have met in several small groups on both the east and west coasts, with those of us near to ACEI headquarters serving as core, sorting with interest the long memoranda and thoughtful comments that traveled up and down and across the country among us by mail. We have subjected each candidate for inclusion to criteria suggested by the Association's Executive Board, to standards developed as Committee action, and to the ideas of each Committee member acting as an individual critic.

A central concern of the Committee was to collect stories that reflect a basic approval of what city life can be, picturing the city not at its grim worst, nor yet as a place of perpetual sweetness and light. We believe the choices indicate city life can be satisfying for a child. These stories represent the richest resource of any city: the vigorous, pulsing variety of its people and their ethnic backgrounds. The games of Maurice and Jacob document the inventiveness of children, Keiko adds to her knowledge of American cats, Lincoln Farnum proves his own resourcefulness, Carlos mitigates destruction, and two little girls delight in kite-flying from a hot tenement rooftop.

It is important that the children are from a variety of racial, ethnic, and religious groups. It is more important that they are lively, resistive to total control, aware of themselves and their fellows, able to accommodate the demands of their surroundings.

Poor children are here, bringing their special gifts of sturdy spirits, faith in their own heritage, and their hope. The not-so-poor are here too. Some have problems unrelated to money; some live an economically limited but far from impoverished life. The amount of family income was not a controlling factor in the choice of these stories.

What the Committee searched for was fiction to give the "feel" of urban life, to suggest the multi-faceted nature of city living, stories free from stereotypes of the city child and the city setting. The Committee has required of each selection that it be rooted in a childlike conception of life in the city and that it have reasonable literary quality, considering its context, its atmosphere, and the theme of the original book from which it was excerpted. Recognizing that nostalgia is more characteristic of adults than children, the Committee has chosen no real period pieces. These are stories of today, with only the pages from *Stuart Little* reminding us what an uncrowded park is like.

The Association and its Committee have several hopes for this collection. First of all, we want it to give pleasure to children: to city children who may recognize themselves and their neighbors, who find new friends in these pages, and who know that tomorrow makes the city more theirs than ours; to country children, who have not seen the city at all, but who can take pleasure in scenery that is unfamiliar, in play that is unlike their own, and in the tantalizing sense that the children in these stories would be fun to know.

Assuming the likelihood that teachers and librarians will use this book with children more often than individual children will take it from the shelves on their own initiative, we hope that leaders of children will find in these stories strong support for their own projects. School and community activities may call for seeking a fresh view for a social studies project, developing an open-ended discussion on citizenship in the city, encouraging creative dramatics, or documenting key elements in our ecosystem; in any of these cases, the resources in this volume can be multiplied by the ingenuity of teachers and community leaders.

Another hope has to do with the books from which these stories were taken. The Committee recognizes that books and excerpts may be uneven in quality. We hope we have done no artistic damage to a writer's creation; we hope we have emphasized no piece out of context. More than anything we hope the taster's feast spread out here will encourage children in their game of private and particular literary exploration, showing them likely subjects to make peculiarly their own. As each city is part of a nation, so each fragment here is part of a book. Some of these books promise exceedingly large rewards for the individual reader, and we wish each of you joy.

One volume could not hold all our favorites, and each member of the Committee regrets at least one gem left out because it was too short or too tight a story to divide, or because some element of the book raised serious objections from a colleague. We did, after all, work as a committee, and what we give you is the *sense* of our meetings, not any final judgment on the "best" of the city stories. The ink may still be wet on stories better than any recorded here; the task of evaluating them, like the cities, belongs ultimately to tomorrow and to the children.

Lois Belfield Watt, Chairman
The Literature Committee

CONTENTS

MAURICE'S ROOM *by Paula Fox* — 1

MR. CHU *by Norma Keating* — 7

A QUIET PLACE *by Rose Blue* — 14

THE STREET OF THE FLOWER BOXES *by Peggy Mann* — 25

WHO'S IN CHARGE OF LINCOLN? *by Dale Fife* — 47

THE CRICKET IN TIMES SQUARE *by George Selden* — 73

MAPLE STREET *by Nan Hayden Agle* — 81

ME AND ARCH AND THE PEST *by John Durham* — 103

NEXT DOOR TO XANADU *by Doris Orgel* — 120

STUART LITTLE *by E. B. White* — 144

THE PROMISED YEAR *by Yoshiko Uchida* — 157

REGGIE'S NO-GOOD BIRD *by Nellie Burchardt* — 173

THE SPIDER PLANT *by Yetta Speevack* — 194

A WONDERFUL, TERRIBLE TIME *by Mary Stolz* — 204

A TRAINFUL OF STRANGERS *by Eleanor Hull* — 243

IT'S LIKE THIS, CAT *by Emily Neville* — 255

ADAM BOOKOUT *by Louisa R. Shotwell* — 275

BIOGRAPHICAL NOTES — 301

MAURICE'S ROOM

by Paula Fox

Maurice was eight and his friend Jacob was seven, and best of all they liked collecting "interesting things." They liked it so well that it was hard to walk in Maurice's room without stepping on something. Maurice's parents threatened to move to the country if Maurice didn't take an interest in better things—like his new trumpet.

"Today you are going to start your trumpet lessons," said Mrs. Henry. She held out a black case that reminded Maurice of a crocodile's head. Maurice put it on his bed and opened it. The trumpet glittered. He could see his face reflected in it.

He looked out of his window. A light rain was falling, a March rain that might be warm. It was exactly the kind of Saturday Maurice and Jacob liked to spend hunting for new things for the collection.

"You'll have to leave very soon," said Mrs. Henry as she started back to the kitchen to finish her cup of coffee. Maurice lifted the snake out of its cage. The snake wound itself around his wrist. It was a dull green color and quite small.

"The trouble with you is you don't have enough interests," he said to the snake. He put it back in its cage and pulled the chicken wire over the top. Then he put on his light jacket.

When he got to the front door, his mother said, "Just a minute. Haven't you forgotten something?" She was holding out the trumpet case. "And Maurice, really! It's raining! Put on your rubbers and your heavy jacket."

"Maurice, you must learn to be more responsible," said his father, who was standing at the other end of the hall eating a piece of whole-wheat toast.

Maurice went back to his room, dug into his closet, and found one of his rubbers and one of Jacob's. He wished he had been born wearing one pair of shoes and one suit of clothes.

Jacob was waiting for him in front of the building.

"Do your lessons really start today?" he asked.

"Yes," said Maurice. As he had guessed, it was a warm spring rain.

"Will you have to go every Saturday morning?"

"For six weeks," said Maurice. "Then they'll see."

"See what?" asked Jacob.

"If I get new interests."

On their way to the music school where Maurice was to take his lesson, they passed a big junk yard. A sign hung over the wire fence that surrounded the yard: *Auto Parts*. A man wearing a hat was walking around the piles of bumpers and tires and car bodies. Now and then he would kick an old fender.

"Why don't you wait for me in there," Maurice suggested. "Maybe you can find something good." The man with the hat walked into a little house not much bigger than a telephone booth. There was a small window in it. Maurice could see the man fiddling with a radio.

"Maybe he'll chase me away," said Jacob, looking at the man.

"I'll stay for a minute," said Maurice.

They walked toward the rear of the lot. The man

looked out of his window but didn't seem to see them. He was chewing on a toothpick and still twisting the radio dials. Just behind the little house, Maurice and Jacob could see the long arm of a crane.

"Look at that!" said Maurice, pointing to a pyramid of heaped-up car parts. Poking out of the pile were hubcaps, fenders, tires, fan belts, radiator caps, pipes, window frames, steering wheels on shafts, and at the very top, lying on a car hood, a pair of headlights that looked almost new.

"We could use those headlights," said Maurice.

Jacob looked back at the little house. "He won't give them to us," he said.

"Maybe he'd make a trade," said Maurice.

"What could we trade?" asked Jacob.

"We'll think of something," Maurice answered. "But first we have to see those headlights."

"How will we get them?" asked Jacob.

"Climb," said Maurice. "See all the places you can put your feet?"

"Me?" asked Jacob.

"I think you can do it better. I'm heavier. If I tried it, everything might crash down," Maurice said.

"Are you going to ask him first if we can?" asked Jacob.

"He's not even looking at us," said Maurice.

Jacob put his right foot on a tire rim, then grabbed

hold of the fender above him and brought his left foot up to another tire. Slowly he climbed toward the top, using the tires as steps.

Suddenly there was a loud clanging of metal, then bangs, screeches, and a crash. When the dust cleared, Maurice saw Jacob almost at the top of the pyramid, stretched out on a silver-colored car hood, clutching its sides.

The man ran out of his little house. When he saw Jacob, he threw his hat on the ground.

"What's the meaning of this!" he shouted.

"We'd like to make a trade," said Maurice.

"Trade! At a time like this?" bellowed the man. "Get off my property!"

"Help!" said Jacob in a weak voice.

"How will we get him down?" asked Maurice.

The man picked up his hat and jammed it back on his head. "Can't he fly?" he growled; then he turned and walked to the crane. He jumped up to the seat and began to push the levers around furiously.

"Don't worry," Maurice called up to Jacob. "He's going to get you down."

Jacob didn't answer. He wasn't scared now, and he rather liked being so high above the ground.

There was a grinding of gears and a maniacal roar as the man maneuvered the crane into position.

"Clear away," shouted the man to Maurice. Maurice

ran back toward the little house and watched as the claw at the end of the cables lowered its jaw, then clamped onto the hood where Jacob lay, gripped it, and lifted it down slowly like a plate. Several tires dislodged by the crane rolled along the ground.

"Well, get up," said Maurice to Jacob. Jacob was feeling sleepy. He shook himself a little and stood up.

"How was it?" asked Maurice.

"Okay," said Jacob.

The man jumped down from the crane, picked up a tire, and kicked it so hard it rolled all the way back to the pile. Then he started toward them.

Maurice and Jacob hurried to the gate. But Maurice stopped suddenly and darted into the little house, where he placed the trumpet on top of the radio.

"It's too late for my lesson anyhow," he said to Jacob as the man yelled after them, "I've got a friend on the police force!"

On the way home, Jacob said, "What will your mother and father say?"

"Plenty!" said Maurice.

MR. CHU

by Norma Keating

Johnny had a job in the Chinese shop of Mr. Lee, who was Mr. Chu's friend too. At night Johnny slept in a place Mr. Lee gave him behind the shop. Whenever he could, Johnny visited Mr. Chu. They cooked Chinese food together, and they saw the city's strange sights together. Then came a special day.

The moon had been right: the wind was not cold in the morning. The brown leaves did a merry, happy dance.

A blade of light fell on Johnny's shoe. The light was

golden, and looked like a great Chinese sword. By noon the sun would be full and warm. Johnny sniffed the air as he walked along. It was filled with spices.

He could smell ginger, nutmeg, and cinnamon. He could smell mustard and garlic, too.

Chinese music floated out of the shops. The musicians were practicing their music. Johnny knew that Chinese music was very old. At first, he used to laugh when he heard it. But when his ears grew accustomed to it, he began to hear sweet, sweet sounds, like seeing a new flower or hearing a new bird from a different town.

Beautiful paper lanterns were strung across the streets. There were lanterns with bright flowers upon them. There were lanterns with little Chinese maidens walking there. They had skin like pale roses and hair as black as night.

There were lanterns with dragons printed on them— golden dragons, red dragons, and some of deep blue.

There were men running in and out of the shops. There were men carrying firecrackers. There were women and children carrying packages. Waiters from the Chinese restaurants were carrying big trays.

There was a movie camera set up to roll. Reporters had come to get the story. Chinese people have celebrated thousands of New Years. The Chinese are a very ancient people.

Johnny could smell the scent of incense sticks. He could smell sweet candy and almonds as he arrived at Mr. Chu's shop. Across the street, a boy dropped a package of firecrackers and bells. He picked them up quickly and ran down the street.

Johnny stood in front of Mr. Chu's shop, and he could hear the music from the inside. Mr. Chu was playing "The General's Song" on the Chinese piano. The piano was flat, like a zither, and had many strings. Mr. Chu played it with long slender wands or sticks. They looked like butterflies hovering over flowers. The strings made a twanging sound. Sometimes it was very sweet. Sometimes it was very loud, like a battle raging. And that was "The General's Song"!

Now the music stopped. Mr. Chu saw Johnny at the door. Mr. Chu wasn't wearing his little leather jacket or his big checkered cap. He had on a long, black silk Chinese New Year's coat. It had little slits up the sides. It was a very nice coat. His neck and smiling face rose out from the high collar.

"Come in, come in. So glad you come early, Johnny."

"Happy New Year, Mr. Chu!"

"You, too, Johnny," said Mr. Chu.

Mr. Chu handed Johnny his Chinese fiddle and bow. Mr. Chu carried the moon. They walked through the busy streets and alleys to Mr. Loo's house.

At Mr. Loo's, many tables had been pushed together to make three long rows. The guests had already arrived. Johnny was seated beside Mr. Chu's uncle.

One by one, waiters with huge trays placed the lovely bowls and serving dishes upon the teakwood table. Inside the dishes there were many delicacies. Mr. Chu called out the names to Johnny:

"Won-ton, Egg Drop, Yat Gaw Mein!
Egg Roll, Bak-toy, Sweet 'n' Sour Pork!
Water Chestnut, Snow Pea, Egg Foo Young!
Roast Duck, Almond Cookie, Fortune Cookie,
    Shrimp!
Ice Cream, Kumquat, Moo Goo Gai Pan!"

Johnny knew that Moo Goo Gai Pan, with its chicken and Chinese vegetables, was Mr. Chu's favorite.

"You eat, Johnny. We make music," said Mr. Chu. First Mr. Chu played the fiddle; then he played upon the moon. Mr. Lee played the Chinese piano, and then he played the horn. Mr. Loo played the happy flute and the sad flute.

"Some White Rose Punch?" said a waiter to the musicians.

"The very same," said Mr. Chu.

"Mandarin tea at the table!"

"The very same," said Mr. Chu.

Johnny's stomach felt as if it would burst, and he had hardly begun to eat! A big mountain of fried rice was before him. "I guess I'd better wait," said Johnny. Mr. Chu saw him, and laughed out loud.

The musicians were playing butterfly notes. These were the little notes that danced around the melody. Mr. Chu played his Chinese fiddle.It had a very long neck with mother-of-pearl flowers and birds on the tip. It had a little round belly with a bridge across it and two strings. The belly of the fiddle rested on his knee instead of under his chin. He drew a bow over it, back and forth like a little saw.

They played "Yankee-Doodle," and "Give My Regards to Broadway," and "You're a Grand Old Flag." Everyone was very happy. Mr. Chu looked at Johnny. He smiled a mysterious smile. Then he began to play "Rain on the Banana Leaves" and "The Most Beautiful Princess." Johnny felt a tingling all over his body. What beautiful music! He nodded his head happily at Mr. Chu.

"Bang, bang, BANG!" the firecrackers popped. It was time to go out into the street. The New Year's celebration had begun!

"Hap—Hap—Happy New Year!" the firecrackers sputtered everywhere.

Johnny stood with Mr. Chu and the musicians. A dancer in a beautiful costume whirled his sharp swords. He charged toward them. Everyone screamed, and Mr. Chu laughed. "He fine dancer, very good actor, too," said Mr. Chu.

Then came the wrestlers. They were as broad and as big as redwood trees. Their legs and thighs were like tree trunks. They had long hair tied in a knot on top of their heads. They grunted and puffed as they wrestled, and everyone shouted and made bets with one another.

"Bang, bang, BANG!" the firecrackers sputtered.

"Here comes the Dragon!" Johnny cried.

Orange flames shot out from the Dragon's green nostrils. He slithered and danced down the street.

"Ehhhhhhh!" screamed the children, with delight.

But Johnny didn't scream. He knew that Chinese men were inside the Dragon, making him slide and walk to and fro. The Dragon snorted, and charged toward the curb. All yellow and scaly and grand was he! "Away, bad spirits!" he seemed to say. "Bring good spirits to the New Year, and happy times ahead."

"Dragon good and kind, Johnny. Fierce too! Dragons hard to find these days," said Mr. Chu.

The lanterns swung in a warm wind above the music

and merriment. The movie cameras clicked away. Up and down and round went the dancers. In and out and away went the Dragon. The street sounds grew softer as the sun went down. The New Year was here to stay.

Mr. Chu turned to Johnny. "You come up to my place for hot tea, Johnny?"

"Thank you, Mr. Chu."

A QUIET PLACE

by Rose Blue

Matthew, black and nine years old, had an unhappy past, but was finding comfort with his generous-spirited foster-parents. He found also a quiet place when he needed it, in the public library—until a day of disturbing news. That afternoon, holding both his book and his trouble tight, he walked slowly up two flights of the five-story house to home.

A delicious smell of something cooking led Matthew into the kitchen where Mama was standing at the stove, stirring a great big pot of stew.

Mama turned, said "Hello, Matthew, honey," and kept stirring without losing the rhythm.

"Hello, Mama," Matthew said quietly. He leaned against the refrigerator awhile, not saying a word.

Mama watched him closely for a long minute. "Anything wrong, Matthew?" she asked.

He shook his head.

"Where you been all day?"

"At the library, Mama," Matthew said softly. "It's closing tomorrow."

Mama stopped stirring. "So that's it," she said, kind of to herself. Then, a little bit louder, she said, "Come over here, sugar."

Matthew walked slowly to the stove and Mama bent down and gave him a great big warm hug. Matthew buried his face against Mama's flowered apron.

"Now," Mama said, "it's not the end of the world. The ladies at the market told me we're getting a library on wheels—a big truck rolling in two times a week. And when the work is all done the new library will be real fine."

Mama took one arm from around Matthew, filled the big wooden stirring spoon with stew and held it to his mouth. "You take a big taste—it'll warm your tummy."

Matthew swallowed the meat and crisp onions and

carrots all mixed together and they went down smooth and warm. He started to feel a little bit better right away.

Footsteps sounded outside the kitchen. When Matthew looked up, Papa was standing there in his blue uniform. Papa was big and strong-looking. He was good to Matthew, but he was tired a lot of the time because he worked so hard delivering people's mail all day.

Papa put his arm around Matthew's shoulder. "Hello, son," he said. "You been a good boy?"

"Yes, Papa," Matthew answered, nodding.

Papa turned to Mama. "Supper ready soon, honey?" he asked.

"Pretty soon now, Papa. Stew has to cook just a little more."

"I'm beat," he said. "Think I'll stretch out awhile. Call me when supper is ready."

"Sure, Papa. You rest yourself. I'll call you." . . .

Matthew promised himself he would get up early, as he did on school days, but next morning Stevie was quiet, and by the time Matthew woke up, Papa had gone to work and Claudia was down with her friends. Mama said, "Sleepyhead, it's near to lunchtime," and she gave him a big meal of hot cereal and bread and jam. After breakfast Matthew got his book and headed for the library. He would be able to finish his book, and after he returned it, there would still be enough time left to think and dream and say goodbye to the children's room and his yellow chair that squished when he sat on it.

As Matthew walked with long steps down the block, Lefty called to him and Matthew turned and waved and said, "Hi, Lefty." Lefty lived four houses down and was in his class at school.

Lefty came up to him and asked, "Where you off to?"

"The library," Matthew said.

"You're a bookworm, man, a real bookworm." Lefty jumped around in front of Matthew, blocking him, and said, "Bookworm, bookworm, bookworm," over and over in a singsong voice.

Matthew said, "Take off, Lefty." He did a little sideways dance step to get out of Lefty's way, and kept going. He didn't want Lefty to think he was running away, so he just took big steps and walked fast.

Lefty had to run to catch up. "Wait up, man, I'll walk you," he said in a friendlier voice.

Matthew and Lefty walked down the block and across the street, walking slow, then fast; then not stepping on the cracks; then one foot in front of the other, balancing on the edge of the curb. They took a short-cut through an alley, stepping over the broken glass, paper, and cans, and came to a vacant lot where a bunch of boys were tossing a ball back and forth.

"Hey," Lefty said, "we've got enough guys for a game."

Quick as a wink the boys found some wood lying in the lot, and before Matthew knew it he was playing first base in a stickball game. He made some great catches, got three hits, including one triple, and his team won in the last half of the ninth inning. Then Matthew picked up his book from the ground, dusted it off, pulled his T-shirt down, and went on to the library.

He climbed the steps just as he had many, many times before and pushed the front door. But this time the door would not open. Matthew pushed harder and harder but still the door stayed closed. Matthew kept pushing and pushing, even though he knew it was no use, even though he knew it was too late, even though he knew the library was closed. Closed for good.

Matthew felt as bad as he had ever felt in his whole life. He sank down onto the stone library steps and just sat there with his chin in his hand. Then he opened the book and read straight through to page 70, to the end, without looking up, without thinking about anything else even for one single second.

He felt glad that things turned out okay for the boy

in the old-time West, but as soon as he closed the book he felt sad all over again. He stared out into space. The stone steps felt hard and he thought of the soft yellow chair that he would never see again.

The click-clack of high heels sounded on the stone, and Matthew felt a hand on his arm. He looked up and there stood a pretty lady with long hair. She looked just like Miss Wilson, his teacher last year, and when she spoke her voice sounded sweet and soft, just like Miss Wilson's did.

"We're closed, dear," she said.

Matthew nodded. "I came to bring back my book," he said sadly, "but I came too late."

The lady sat down beside Matthew, right on the steps, as if she didn't even care about dirtying her dress.

"You can return your book tomorrow, you know," she said. "The bookmobile will come every Friday and every Tuesday, and it will be here tomorrow from eleven in the morning till three in the afternoon. It's a real library in a great big truck. Won't that be nice?"

Matthew nodded because he could tell she wanted to cheer him up, but he knew the bookmobile wouldn't be the same. Not the same at all. A truck that came and went away couldn't be like a big brick library that stood in the same place all the time and was there when you needed it. . . .

When Matthew woke the next morning he found that Mama had gone to the store, as she did every Friday, and that today Claudia was staying home to mind Stevie. She fixed cold cereal for Matthew, and after breakfast he took his book and told Claudia that he was going to the new bookmobile.

Claudia laughed and said, "You gonna find something in those books of yours that'll do us any good?" But Matthew just looked away without answering. Claudia rumpled his hair and said, "You take care, hear?" and Matthew went off to return his book.

On the corner, one block away from the closed library, Matthew saw the long green bookmobile. He walked up to the truck, climbed the three little steps, and walked inside. A girl who looked a little like Claudia took his book from him. The pretty lady from the library was standing next to her, stamping books for people to take home. She smiled when she saw Matthew and said, "You look around, dear. I'll come over as soon as I can and help you find a book you'll like."

Matthew smiled back and walked around the bookmobile, looking for the children's section. There were other people walking around too, and they were all close together because there wasn't a lot of room. The books were lined up against the wall on shelves and when you walked behind cubbies and around them you couldn't find a place to be by yourself. Matthew saw that he couldn't stay at the bookmobile the way he could at a real library. So when he came to the children's section he looked through the shelves and tried to find a book as fast as he could. He looked at the titles and all the bright book covers till his eyes fell on a book with a picture of a boy on it. The boy had brown skin just like Matthew's and he looked about the same age. Matthew thought it would be nice to read a book about a boy who looked so much like himself, so he picked it up and took it to the lady, and she said, "You picked out a good book all by yourself." Then she took his card and stamped the book.

Matthew wanted to start his book right away, so he walked straight home. When he got there, Mama was putting groceries away. She hugged him and said, "Hello, sugar," and he hugged her back, took a handful of grapes from the open bag in the sink, and went to his room with his brand-new book.

After he looked at the picture of the boy on the front cover, Matthew turned the book over to look at the back cover. Just then Stevie woke from his nap and began to howl. Mama came in to see what was wrong. She picked up the baby and held him, but he kept howling and howling. She put him on the floor and he took a few steps, but then he fell down and howled some more.

Matthew picked up his book and took it to the bath-room. He locked the door, sat down, and looked at the back cover. There were pictures of some houses on a street that looked like his street. Matthew had never seen a picture like that before, not on the cover of any book he had read, and he was still looking at it when Claudia banged on the door.

"Hey," she yelled. "You staying there all day? Roy's coming pretty soon and I've got to get ready."

Matthew took his book, left the bathroom, and went out the front door. He stood outside for a few minutes, just leaning against the door, and then he climbed the stairs, all the way to the roof. He pushed open the heavy door and stepped onto the tar-covered floor. Three ladies were hanging clothes on the line and talk-ing, and in a corner two big boys were sitting, playing a radio very loud. The roof was no better for reading and sitting quiet than home was, so Matthew went down again, down all the steps and out to the street.

He went up and down the streets, in and out of al-leys, searching for a quiet place. But he found none. His school was across the avenue and down three blocks. He walked by it and wandered around till he came to the park. He passed mothers with baby car-riages, children playing in the playground, big kids playing ball. He crossed a path, and kept going until he saw a high, sloping, grassy hill near the back of the park.

He climbed up to the top, where there was a great big leafy tree with four smaller trees around it. The trunk of the big tree made a chair and Matthew sat on it. When he looked down he saw people walking on the path, but they looked far away, and he could hardly hear them. When he looked up he saw a ceiling of leaves with little patches of sky and sunlight showing through.

He sat there, just watching the breeze move the leaves around, till a stronger chill wind came and made the leaves shudder as the sun hid behind a dark cloud. A shiver ran through him, and though the wind stopped and the sun came out once more, Matthew felt no warmer. It was almost autumn, and after autumn came winter and the snow would cover his tree. Winter would come and where would he go?

Matthew huddled against his tree trunk, holding his book, and then he thought of another boy, the boy in the book he had just finished, the boy who lived way out west, a long, long time ago. He thought how that boy had gone looking for new places and traveled far when the way was hard. Yet the little boy kept looking even though the winter was bitter cold. The little boy in the West was hungry lots of times and had to find his own food. Matthew felt lucky—it was still summer now, with time to look for a new place and still be warm. And tomorrow Matthew's mama would give him a great, big, hot breakfast. Tomorrow, right after breakfast, Matthew would go place-hunting. He would find a quiet place and have it all ready for winter. He would start with his own basement, and if that wasn't right, he'd search on. He had found an outside place. He could find an inside one. And then after autumn and winter, spring would come round again and Matthew could come back to his tree.

Matthew rolled over on his tummy and lay flat on the soft grass. He put his book down on the ground with the front cover facing him, and with his finger he traced the picture of the boy. Then he leaned his elbow on the grass, rested his chin on his hand, and opened to page 1.

THE STREET OF THE FLOWER BOXES

by Peggy Mann

"Look!" cried little Luis, pointing.

Carlos looked. Something was happening *again* at the New House. This time a truck had parked in front of it; a truck filled with flowers!

The two brothers ran up the street and stood watching as a fat man in overalls hefted a huge bush down the steps and into the areaway of the New House. Then, returning to the truck, he lifted out a long wooden tray filled with flower pots. He set these out carefully beside the bush, and the brick-paved areaway was transformed into a sudden field of flowers.

"*Caramba!*" little Luis exclaimed with some excitement. "I wonder what's goin' on at this New House *now!*"

Actually, the New House was as old as any of the other brownstone buildings on West Ninety-fourth Street. In fact, for a time it had looked even sadder than the rest of the rundown roominghouses. That was after the fire. All the people had moved out. The broken windows stared like blind eyes. And when the boys on the block climbed inside the building hoping to find a place for a clubhouse, they saw that floorboards had been burned through. Ceiling beams were charred and blackened. And the stinging smell of smoke still hung about the empty rooms.

Then one bright blue morning in April a crew of workmen had arrived at the house: plumbers, plasterers, painters, carpenters. Trucks started pulling up outside to deposit piles of sand, lumber, cement blocks, bricks, bathroom tiles, and all shapes and sizes of wooden boxes and cardboard cartons marked with such words as ELECTRICAL FIXTURE or AUTOMATIC DISHWASHER.

Finally, on the first day of June a gigantic moving van arrived. And the children of the block gathered round to watch men carrying from the van the finest furniture which had ever been seen on West 94th Street.

Then a lady and a man drove up in a taxi and entered the house.

"They sure got a pretty new landlady!" Luis had remarked to his brother.

It was after the lady and man moved in that changes began to occur on the outside of the house. Bright blue shutters edged the windows. Two old-fashioned lanterns framed the front door. And three low brick troughs were built along the side of the areaway. The children made bets as to what these troughs were for.

"To keep goldfishes in," Clarence suggested.

"Some fancy new kinda garbage cans," Carlos had said.

Now, however, the mystery was solved. The man from the flower truck filled the brick troughs with dirt. Then he started planting. Bushes and small trees. Long strands of ivy. And finally an assortment of blossoms which, he told the boys, were called petunias.

"*Petooonias?*" Carlos said. "What kinda nutty name is that? Petooonias Spitooonias!"

The other children who had come to watch laughed loudly.

"*I* think they're pretty!" little Luis said. But he was only five years old and small for his age and no one ever took any notice of his remarks. He was tolerated, in fact, only because he was Carlos' brother.

Carlos was nine. Carlos was tough. Carlos was the leader of the boys still too young to become members of the Big Kings, the official block gang.

At times even the Big Kings had been known to follow Carlos' leadership. Especially when he invented games. Walking the Plank, for example. One day he had taken a large beam of wood from the pile of lumber outside the New House. He laid it across the top of two parked cars, and a pirate blindfold was tied over the eyes of each block boy as he teetered his way carefully across the plank. Silly Annello fell off and broke his left arm in three places. But everyone expected something like that from Silly.

Carlos had also invented The Traffic Tieup. Having heard the term on the radio so often, he'd decided to try it out on West 94th Street. He and Clarence collected all manner of clotheslines and ropes. When night came the block boys had a fine time tying ropes from the fender of one car to the door handle of another, parked across the street. The result was a Traffic Tieup with such splendid honking and shouting that two squad cars of armed and helmeted policemen were sent rushing to 94th Street.

Now Carlos invented another game.

When the flower man had driven off in his truck, Carlos shouted, "Let's play Cat-a-Nine-Tails!"

He promptly pulled out one of the long strands of ivy and slung it about his head like a lariat, hitting Eddie in the face with the ivy roots. Some of the dirt went in Eddie's mouth which was open wide with laughter. Eddie began to cry.

"Whatchu doin'!" Clarence hollered. He was Eddie's older brother. *He* pulled a long strand of ivy from the brick trough, circled it around his head, and banged the roots into little Luis' face.

Then the Battle of the Ivy began. It was followed by the Rain of the Petunia Petals. And when there was nothing left to throw, the boys broke branches from the bushes and tiny trees and chased each other up and down the block screaming with laughter.

The women sitting out on the brownstone stoops, and the men playing dominoes or dice on the sidewalk, watched the boys and laughed along with them. That fine Lady and Gentleman would sure have a fit when they got home and looked into their flower boxes! And it would serve them right. Rich people could do as they wished, of course. But at least they should have sense enough not to show off by moving right in among the poor!

At five-thirty that evening the adults on the block as

well as the children were sitting out on the brownstone steps waiting with anticipation until the lady got home. She and the man went off to work every morning. But the lady usually came home first, carrying a bag of groceries.

And sure enough, at five-thirty she arrived. The people of the block kept talking as usual, pretending not to notice her. But all voices fell to a hush as the lady started up the front steps of the New House. Then she glanced into the areaway.

"Goodness!" she said.

She stood for a long moment looking at the pulled-up ivy, the broken branches, the bent flower stalks, the crazy pattern of pink, white, blue, and red flower petals crushed against the brick floor of the areaway. Then she glanced at the people sitting on the steps of the neighboring stoop. "Do you know who—did all this?" she asked of no one in particular.

The people stared back at her, impassive.

Finally, Mr. Gonzales said, "*No se, señora.*" Mr. Gonzales had been born in Manhattan and knew perfect English. But he answered the lady in Spanish which she obviously did not understand. She smiled a little, or rather she stretched her mouth in a strained, polite kind of way. Then she went on into her house. And shut the door behind her.

Immediately, the street broke into its usual hubbub of sound. The bongo drums began. Mothers leaned out of upstairs windows to call their children. And the general hum of conversation rose like a wall from the people who sat on the stoop steps which, in the spring and summertime, were as crowded as World Series bleachers. On this evening the conversation rose even louder than usual as people reported to each other from stoop to stoop on what the lady had said when she saw her flower boxes.

It was also reported up and down the street that Carlos Gomez and *his* kids had done the damage. No one seemed to blame Carlos; it was simply a part of the News.

The report, however, came to the ears of Carlos' grandmother, who stuck her head out the window to learn what the new commotion was all about. His grandmother was a strict old lady, related in some vague way to a wealthy Puerto Rican landowner. She was proud of her heritage and tried to bring up her two grandsons to be gentlemen. She was reasonably pleased with little Luis. But she cringed inwardly at each report of Carlos' wrongdoings. Outwardly, she reacted by hitting him frequently with a ruler.

The ruler was ready now when Carlos came in for supper. He got a dozen swift strokes on each palm.

The strokes were not hard ones, but they were accompanied by a shrilling of Spanish severity from the grandmother. Then Carlos was told that he must go at once and apologize to the lady for what he had done. Otherwise, he would not get any supper this night, or any other night.

"Listen, Grandmother," Carlos complained. "The flowers were bound to be pulled up by *some*one! That nutty lady should have more sense. Who plants *flowers* on this crummy street?"

His grandmother, who knew little English, did not understand what Carlos had said. Nor did she care. "*Anda!*" she said, pointing at the door. "Go!"

Carlos went.

He was not exactly afraid as he rang the highly polished brass bell of the New House. But he fervently hoped it would be the lady who answered the door, not the man.

It was the man.

"Hi," Carlos said, looking up. The man seemed much taller than usual.

"Hello," the man said.

"I come to tell," Carlos mumbled, wanting to get it over quickly, "I'm sorry about the flowers."

"Yes," the man said. "So am I. I wonder who did it."

Carlos shrugged one shoulder. Then he shrugged the other shoulder.

"Do you think," the man said, "if we order some more flowers *they* will be ripped up too?"

Carlos shrugged both shoulders at once, and flipped out his hands. "People on this crummy block are not used to nice flowers."

"I suppose we could put up a fence," the man said. "To keep the kids out of our areaway."

The lady had come to the door and the man put his arm around her shoulders. "I don't like fences," she said suddenly. "Anyway, it seems to me fences were made to be climbed by children. Right?" Surprisingly, she smiled at Carlos.

He nodded.

"If we get some more flowers," the lady said to Carlos, "would you be their—guardian?"

Carlos frowned, rather suspicious. "What's—guardian?"

"Well," she said, "kind of a mixture of gardener and guard. Part of the job would be to water the boxes three times a week. But the main thing would be protecting the plants. This time we'd get little seedlings. They're not so expensive as the full-grown flowers.

You'd have to see that nothing or nobody harmed them so they can grow big. Like the ones we had."

"Your pay," the man added, "would be a quarter a week."

Carlos stared at him.

"Well?" the man said. "How about it?"

Once more Carlos shrugged. "Sure. Why not?"

"What's your name?" the man asked.

"Carlos Gomez."

"We're the Mitchells," the man said. "We'll be seeing you, Carlos."

They shook hands.

Carlos turned, ran down the steps of the brownstone stoop and up the block to his own house. He began to whistle. Not only had he been spared the shame of apologizing, but he had made a deal which would net him a quarter a week. In addition, his grandmother would no doubt be so pleased at the news of his guardian job that she would give him an extra dessert for dinner.

Then, however, another thought hit him. The Big Kings! What would they have to say about it? Especially Angel Andino, their leader. Maybe it would cancel out his future with the Kings, if he took on this crazy job. Protecting *flowers!* He could just hear the Kings laughing over *that!*

He decided not to accept the job. After all, his future with the Kings was more important than a lousy quarter a week. (Even though—he reflected quite often—a quarter could buy enough candy to eat yourself sick on. And Carlos was very partial to candy.)

The following Saturday morning, after watching the City Gardener truck arrive and leave, he marched up the steps of the New House determined to tell the Mitchells they had better find someone else to be guardian of their flowers.

The lady opened the door, and gave him that same wide smile.

"Hi!" she said. "Just on time. The plants have arrived. And this too. Your equipment!" She handed him a large aluminum watering can.

Carlos took it.

"If you're free now," the lady said, "let's start in planting the seedlings. Okay?"

Carlos was silent.

"*Are* you free now?" she said. "Otherwise we could do it later in the day."

There was a long pause.

"Is anything—wrong, Carlos?"

He remembered the look on her face when she had first seen her torn-up flower boxes. Somehow he didn't want to ever see her look like that again.

"Sure, lady," he told her. "*Bueno vamos!* That's Spanish," he explained, "for let's get going!"

Some of the kids on the block came around to watch him and the lady do the planting. Certain remarks were made in Spanish. But the lady didn't understand. And Carlos didn't translate.

He did, however, inform the bystanders that he planned to "get" anyone who disturbed the flowers. This remark too was made in Spanish.

"What did you tell them?" the lady said.

"Told them to clear off!" He repeated this sentence in somewhat stronger Spanish words; and with a few further jibes and shoulder shrugs the children moved off. The sidewalk was empty.

The lady had gone inside and Carlos was alone watering down the tiny seedlings and the ivy when Angel Andino appeared. He stood watching for a time in silence. Then he said, "Man, you kill me! Your little silver watering can and all!"

"Listen," Carlos told him, defiant, "if you were given a quarter a week to slop some water on some ol' weeds, would you turn it down?"

"I got a lot better ways to get me a quarter a week," Angel said. Then he walked away.

Carlos watched him sauntering off down the street.

There was no way to protect the plants if the Big Kings decided to get them.

Each morning when he woke, Carlos ran to the window. He could see the brick flower boxes from there. And each morning he gave an invisible sigh. The ivy was still in place. No one had disturbed the plants.

It was the same thing at school. Toward the end of the day he got restless, jumpy, wondering whether the Kings had decided to destroy his plants. When the bell rang he would be out of his seat and through the door while the echoes of the schoolbell-clanging were still sounding in the air. And each afternoon he found that his boxes were fine. It seemed like a kind of miracle.

Maybe it was due to the licorice shoelaces.

When Carlos received his first quarter's wages he inquired of Pepe, Angel's little brother, whether Angel liked candy and, if so, what kind.

"Licorice," Pepe said. "Those long twisty kind. Called shoelaces. They really turn him on!"

So Carlos went into Mr. Moriority's candy store on the corner and purchased ten cents' worth of licorice shoelaces which he presented to Pepe.

"For Angel," he said carefully. "With my compliments."

The remaining fifteen cents went for the purchase of assorted sucking and chewing candies which—as a further insurance—he shared with the smaller children on the street.

The system seemed to work, for the flowers remained unmolested.

Furthermore, they grew!

That was the real miracle. In this street littered with the overflow from garbage pails, torn newspapers, and empty cans, these tiny seedlings slowly stretched up green and tall, and sprouted flowers! Just like they were in the fresh-air country someplace. They sprouted and budded like crazy and made fresh new blossoms all through the summer.

What with his high expenses for protection payoffs, Carlos didn't make much profit as gardener. But in fact he didn't mind much. His flowers were doing fine.

Sometimes Clarence and Eddie and others asked if they could help him tend the brick boxes. But Carlos said firmly, "No!" He felt that he knew each flower and ivy plant personally; each one needed the special care and attention he gave it.

In July his Cousin José-from-the-Bronx came to stay while José's mother was in the hospital having another new baby. Carlos and Luis took him on a tour of the neighborhood showing off the special sights. Saving the best for the last. They stopped finally by the brick flower boxes at the New House.

"My brother's the gardener at this place!" little Luis announced proudly.

"Yeah?" José said, impressed. He looked at Carlos, who shrugged one shoulder in a modest way.

José-from-the-Bronx stroked one of the pink petunia petals.

"Hey!" Carlos put out a restraining hand. "Stop it, Stupid! Don't you know it'd kill the flowers if everyone started feeling them and pinching them all the time?"

"I wish I could be a gardener," José remarked rather wistfully.

"Me too!" said little Luis.

"You can!"

The three boys looked up to see who had spoken.

It was the lady. She was standing by the open window watching them. She smiled. "Come up here, boys. My husband and I would like to discuss something with you."

Carlos went first, marching confidently up the steps of the brownstone stoop. Luis and José followed, holding hands.

It was the first time any of the block children had been inside the New House. At first they just stood still, looking around. There was a piano in the corner. There was a fireplace. A whole wall made of books.

"What's *that* thing?" Carlos said finally, pointing at

a bush of glass icicles which hung upside down from the ceiling.

"A chandelier," the lady said. She flicked a wall switch and tiny light bulbs glowed from some of the icicles.

Carlos nodded approvingly. "Pretty good," he said. "Only it doesn't give much light."

The lady laughed. "Well, that's true. But you can't have everything. Sit down, boys," she said. "I'll get my husband."

They sat, lined up stiffly on the edge of the soft red sofa.

The lady went to the foot of the stairs. "Peter," she called. "We have some visitors."

When the man came down he settled back in the armchair and lit his pipe. "Well," he said, "here's our proposition. It seems that some of the flowers and ivy in the areaway boxes will have to be transplanted into window boxes."

The three boys nodded, though none was quite certain what *transplant* meant.

"As it happens," the man said, "Julie—my wife—and I had already ordered more flowers and ivy for our own window boxes before we thought of this transplanting idea. Our order is arriving today. But if you boys think it's a good plan, I could ring up and get a few extra window boxes. You can transplant some of the flowers and ivy from the areaway. Then each of you can be the gardener for your own window box on your own windowsill. How does that strike you?"

"Sounds okay," Carlos said. (Perhaps his grandmother would know the meaning of *transplant*. But he doubted it, since she knew very little English at all.)

"Well, I'll go telephone City Gardener for the extra boxes," the man said. "That way we'll have yours this afternoon when they deliver our order."

When the man had left, Carlos whispered something in Spanish to little Luis. And Luis immediately piped up, "Lady, my brother say to ask you what means transplant."

"I don't say to ask for *me*," Carlos explained, reddening. "I thought *they* maybe don't know." He indicated the two younger boys. "And you are better to explain, lady, than me."

"First of all," the lady said, smiling, "my name is Mrs. Mitchell. Or Julie. Not lady."

"Sure, lady," Carlos said. "I understand."

"Well," she went on, explaining it only to Luis and José, "this is what *transplant* means. Take our petunia seedlings, for example. They all grew big and strong. None of them died—which might have happened if they hadn't had such expert care from Carlos."

Luis looked at his brother and grinned with pride. Carlos shrugged one shoulder in a modest manner.

"However," the lady continued, "because *all* the flowers grew so well, the box is now too overcrowded. Some of the smaller plants can't get enough sun or enough nourishment. And they may die."

Luis looked at his brother again, and frowned. Had Carlos done something *wrong?*

But the lady went on in a cheerful voice. "So the thing to do is what all the best gardeners do. Dig out some of the petunias very carefully by the roots and replant them in new window boxes of their own where they'll have plenty of space to grow. And where they can get all the special attention they need from *their* gardeners."

"And that's what is called transplant!" Carlos concluded turning to his brother and cousin, as though he had given the entire lecture.

Mr. Mitchell returned to the room. "Okay!" he announced. "It's all set. City Gardener will be along this afternoon. Suppose you boys ring my bell when you see the truck in the street and we'll get to work."

"Sure!" Carlos said as they rose to go. "Then we will make the transplant."

It was three o'clock when the truck filled with potted flowers and ivy pulled up outside the New House. At one minute past three Carlos, Luis, and José climbed the stoop steps. They had carefully kept the secret of the transplanting from the other boys on the block. "Otherwise," Carlos explained, "they'll all want window boxes. And there's not enough transplants to go around."

He was also worried about Angel Andino. Maybe the Big Kings had come to like the look of flowers on their street. Maybe if they saw some extra boxes being made, they'd want them.

"Now, what we got to do," Carlos warned, "is get our boxes onto our own windowsills before those punks is any the wiser!"

He put his finger on the polished brass bell of the New House, and rang.

Mr. Mitchell opened the door and let them in. "Look, boys," he said, "my wife had still another idea. The plastic window boxes which come from City Gardener are all the same shade of green. Julie would like ours painted blue to match our window shutters. I've ordered six boxes for this house. Would you fellows care to do the painting?"

The three heads nodded.

"They'll have to be very carefully done," Mr. Mitchell said. "The pay," he added, "will be twenty-five cents a box. Okay?"

Again, the boys nodded. "The best of anything I

love to do," little Luis exclaimed, "is painting! I never done it before," he added.

Meanwhile, the City Gardener man had deposited in the areaway: four large baskets of earth, eighteen pots of red geraniums, six pots of pink geraniums, twenty-four pots of long, dangling English ivy, and nine green plastic window boxes.

The lady gave the boys a pile of old newspapers which they spread carefully over the remaining floor space of the areaway. Then she supplied them with three brushes, a large half-filled can of blue paint and a bottle of turpentine.

They began busily to paint six of the green boxes blue.

The secret of course could be kept no longer. Almost immediately, it seemed, every small child in the block had gathered by the areaway of the New House. Even Chico and Ramon, two of the Kings, stopped by to make some sneering comments. But they too stayed to watch.

"We're gonna transplant!" little Luis announced proudly and loudly to no one in particular.

"What's transplant?" Eddie inquired.

"What's the matter?" Carlos straightened up. A streak of blue paint ran from his ear down to his chin. He glared at the gathered crowd. "You don't even know what transplant means? And you supposed to know *English*?"

After that most of the block boys wandered away. Including Chico and Ramon. Maybe because even *they* didn't know the meaning of transplant. They rejoined the stickball game the Kings were playing in the street.

When the three painters had finished their job and had wiped their hands and faces reasonably clean with turpentine-soaked rags, they went inside for their pay and—as it turned out—for lemonade and sandwiches.

"You know, I been thinking," Carlos remarked as he finished off a peanut butter sandwich. "My favorite color is yellow. Maybe I'll use my twenty-five cents pay to buy me some paint so as I can make my green plastic window box yellow."

"That's a wonderful idea!" the lady said.

"Me, I think I'll paint my window box white!" José said. "White is the cleanest-lookin' color there is."

"I'm having pink!" little Luis announced. "To match my pink geraniums."

"*What* pink geraniums?" Carlos asked.

"There's pink ones. Six pink ones!" Luis insisted. "Outside in the areaway. I counted."

"They're for the lady and man!" Carlos said. "The ones we transplant will all be petunias. Right, lady?"

"Right," she said. "And wrong. We only have petunias in the areaway. You're right there, Carlos. But my husband and I have decided that we would like some petunias in our window boxes. So if it's all right with you, Carlos, we'll trade some of the geraniums and ivy which came today, in return for some of your transplanted petunias."

"Sure," Carlos replied, rather grandly. "That's okay." He turned to his brother. "There," he said. "Now you can have a couple of pink geraniums if you want to!"

WHO'S IN CHARGE OF LINCOLN?

by Dale Fife

No one believed the things that happened to Lincoln.

Not his big sister Sara.

Not his middle-sized sisters, Sassy and Sissy.

Even Pop sometimes raised an eyebrow at Lincoln's stories.

Mom always listened with a serious face to whatever Lincoln had to tell.

But Mom had to leave suddenly for the hospital

early this morning to bring home the new baby who it seemed was joining the Farnums two days early.

This put the family smack in the middle of the emergency Pop had worried about, and now no one believed Lincoln when he announced that a horse had fallen on Mrs. Readywell.

Pop had the family organized and running as smoothly as his railroad. "Always start with a clear track, and an eagle-eyed engineer who knows how to get where he's going," was his favorite advice. Before Pop left last night on his New York-to-Chicago run, he wrote out Emergency Orders.

So here they were, the four Farnums, lined up in the kitchen like a string of boxcars, with Sara the acting "Eagle Eyes." Her voice, as she read Pop's instructions, was real bossy:

"In case your mother should go to the hospital while I'm away, Sassy and Sissy are to go straight to Aunt Charlotte's from school, with NO BRANCHING OFF the main line. They are to stay until I get home so Sara will be free to go with her class to Washington."

Sassy and Sissy jumped up and down, excited about staying overnight at Aunt Charlotte's.

Lincoln thought about Sara going to Washington, Mr. Lincoln's city. Pop and Mom had gone a year ago.

So had Uncle Jay. They still talked about it. What stories they told. Lincoln liked to listen to them.

And Sara was going there this very day. She was in charge of the family this morning and acting as important as a switch engine in a roundhouse, but just the same her eyes danced and she looked pretty in her best dress.

"May I go with you, Sara?" Lincoln asked, knowing the answer full well.

"Of course not," the know-it-all twin, Sassy, flared. "It's mostly high school students who get to go in a group. You're just a little third-grader. Much too young."

"I'm not," Lincoln protested.

"Who's in charge of Lincoln?" Sissy, the curious twin, asked.

"If you'll all hush," Sara said, "I'll read the rest of the instructions:

"Lincoln is to come home from school as usual. Mrs. Readywell will be here."

"Why doesn't Lincoln go with us?" Sissy asked.

"Because he's a boy and Aunt Charlotte has only girls and boys make her nervous," Sara said. "Especially boys who get lost for hours on end."

"I wasn't lost that time at Aunt Charlotte's," Lincoln said. "I was up on the apartment roof looking through my telescope, watching the people on Mars."

Sara sighed and went on talking. "Mrs. Readywell was coming anyway to stay while Mom was in the hospital. Pop asked her to come earlier, just in case. Won't she be surprised when she gets here today and finds Mom's already left?"

Lincoln raised his voice once more. "A horse fell on Mrs. Readywell."

Sissy giggled. "Lincoln's dreaming again."

"It's his imagination blasting off," Sassy said. "Ten . . . nine . . . eight . . ."

"Quiet, everyone," Sara ordered. "It's time to get yourselves ready for school."

Girls! Lincoln thought. You just couldn't tell them anything. They knew it all. Well, there was one thing they didn't know. A horse *did* fall on Mrs. Readywell.

In his room, which was at the front of the apartment, Lincoln stuffed his books into his book bag. He made his bed, pounding the lumps flat with his fists, and he straightened the statue of Mr. Lincoln which stood on his bookshelf.

Mr. Lincoln was his special friend. It was true that Lincoln sometimes mixed the real with the dreams. Living in a house noisy with girl talk, he had to. Now Mr. Lincoln was real, but not real-real like this red brick apartment. It wasn't a big apartment house, just three floors with two families on each floor. Some of the older people called it a flat, and it stood in a long row of buildings all just like it. The rooms marched in a straight line like a string of cars on Pop's railroad, and so Lincoln sometimes pretended he was on a train.

Lincoln knew about trains because Pop talked to him about his work. Just last month Pop took him on the subway to the railroad station and showed him all around the yards, and let him climb aboard and walk through a mainline passenger train, from one end to the other.

Lincoln looked out the window onto the street and saw that the fat girl with the long braids was twisting again. Now, *she* was real. She was the very last of the hoopers on the block. Whenever Lincoln looked out the window she was there twisting in her red hoop.

The girls having a quick game of hopscotch before school in the spring sunshine, they were real, and the boys bouncing a ball off the sooty flat across the street. And Officer Roberts, talking with the ladies on the stoop across the street, he was real.

The telephone call from Mrs. Readywell this morning was real too. Mom had come out into the kitchen with her coat and hat on, and carrying a little suitcase. Sara had rushed out to hail a cab. Everyone had been excited and gone with Mom out to the street and helped her into the cab. She was giving all kinds of last-minute instructions: "Lincoln, you be polite to Mrs. Readywell; Sara, you call Aunt Charlotte, and be careful in Washington; Sissy and Sassy, you mind Aunt Charlotte . . ."

In all the confusion, with the cab pulling away from the curb and everyone shouting good-bye, Lincoln was the only one who heard the telephone ring. As soon as he answered, Mrs. Readywell began talking as if he were Mom: "A sawhorse fell on me while I was painting the bathroom just now. It was standing on end in the corner and it toppled over and broke my glasses. It's not enough that I have a tin ear; now I can't see either. So I won't be able to come today because I have to get new glasses. I'll be there tomorrow afternoon, and don't you get any ideas about going to the hospital early."

Mrs. Readywell had hung up before Lincoln could tell her that Mom was already on the way to the hospital. It wouldn't have done any good anyway. Mrs. Readywell couldn't hear well and a conversation with her was just one-way.

Across the street now Officer Roberts smiled good-bye to the ladies on the stoop and headed for the subway corner. Lincoln slung his book bag over his shoulder and ran the length of the apartment from the engine to the caboose. . . .

After school, Lincoln shot a few baskets out behind the apartment, but it was no fun with nobody watching.

He decided to go out front where there was more excitement.

He sat on the stoop for a while, then he walked to the corner, past some girls playing jump-the-rope, and more girls showing off on roller skates. It felt good to be on his own without his sisters bossing him, telling him to change his clothes, or go wash his face, or something.

Of course, later, when he was sure Uncle Jay was home from work he'd have to telephone Aunt Charlotte's. He'd talk to Uncle Jay and tell him the whole story about Mrs. Readywell. It would be different from telling it to Aunt Charlotte, who got excited over the least little thing Lincoln said. Uncle Jay would come over and maybe sleep in Pop's bed, but first they'd shoot a few baskets and Uncle Jay would show Lincoln once more just how he had made that champion shot. But Uncle Jay wouldn't be home from work for quite a while yet.

Lincoln crossed the street. He walked past the Savings and Loan Bank on the corner, past the delicatessen and the Laundromat. He stopped in front of the grocery store and leaned against the window. He felt so free he thought he could fly. He was an eagle soaring high as a jet. He pumped his arms up and down and the wind and clouds brushed his face.

At that moment, a man, with his coat collar turned up and his hat brim turned down, came hurrying down the street. He tossed a brown paper sack into Lincoln's outstretched wings, and shoved some bills into his fist. "There's more where this came from if you'll take my lunch to the subway corner and wait for me," the man said over his shoulder as he flashed out of sight in the crowd.

Lincoln clutched the bag and looked at the money. The man had given him three five-dollar bills. *Zowie!* Lincoln took off like a fire engine. Behind him he heard a clatter of bells. When he was halfway down the street a police car screamed by.

At the subway stairs Lincoln waited and waited.

After a while, Officer Roberts arrived, all business and no nonsense, the way he was when he had no time for jokes. "What you hanging around for, son?" he asked.

"I'm waiting for a man to pick up his lunch," Lincoln said, holding up the sack.

"Well, it's way past lunchtime," Officer Roberts said. "Now you get along home."

Pop was a stickler about doing exactly as Officer Roberts said, so Lincoln went home.

He let himself into the house, walked to the kitchen and plunked the sack down on the table. It began to split. Before his eyes, bundles of greenbacks spilled on the table.

Was he dreaming? Lincoln closed his eyes, then opened them slowly.

He was surrounded by money.

He took three steps forward, then three steps sideways, and looked again.

It was still money.

Zowie! What would Officer Roberts say about this?

Quickly, he emptied his book bag and stuffed the money, torn sack and all, into it. Then he highballed it out of the house. He did remember to put the key back.

At the subway corner, Officer Roberts was untangling traffic. Lincoln held up the bag. "It's filled with money," he cried.

Officer Roberts was having troubles. He was blowing his whistle at a lady jaywalker, and at the same time he was trying to stop a dogfight. A police car whined down the street and stopped right next to him.

"Officer Roberts . . ." Lincoln cried. "Officer Roberts."

Officer Roberts waved Lincoln away. "Now see here, young man. I'm too busy to listen to your yarns today.

Away with you and don't you dare let me catch you back here again."

Well! Money belonged in a bank, Lincoln knew that. It must be almost closing time. He raced down the street and around the corner. A guard was just pulling the doors closed.

Lincoln held up the bag. "It's money."

The guard shrugged, pointed to the closing time on the window, and pulled down the shade.

Lincoln stopped to think. What should he do now? If he took the money to Aunt Charlotte's she'd probably faint. Still, he couldn't just walk around with it, waiting for Uncle Jay to get home from work.

Now, if only Sara were here. He was used to her being in charge when Pop and Mom were not at home. She was bossy but she did know the right thing to do.

But Sara was on her way to Washington.

No, she wasn't! Not yet! Her train wasn't to leave until sometime after school was out. If he rushed to the station he'd probably be just in time to see her.

As he made a dash for the subway stairs, Lincoln saw that Officer Roberts was busier than ever. He was talking with two policemen now. They pointed this way and that. They shook their heads. They wrote things down.

Lincoln knew about subways. Often on Sundays after church Pop took the family to places like the United Nations or Rockefeller Center. Always, he gave the children the money to pay the fares. It was more fun that way.

So Lincoln knew how to get places. He went to the change booth and with one of the five-dollar bills he bought some tokens, then dropped one in the turnstile, and swung aboard the subway.

The Washington train was being called when Lincoln burst into the station. He rushed this way and that, skidding over the floor, looking for Sara. He remembered that she was wearing a blue dress this morning so he chased after every blue dress in sight. But Sara just wasn't around anywhere. Well, he thought, it was just like her to have been the very first one to board the train.

Over the loudspeaker now he heard the last call for the Washington train. He squirreled through the line headed for the gate, peering up into faces. He was carried along by the crowd right through the gate and, for goodness sakes, there was the train. He sprinted onto the last car and rushed from coach to coach looking for Sara. He reached the very last one, a real old-timer. But Sara wasn't in Old-Timer either. Come to think about it, Lincoln hadn't seen any sign of a high school group on the train.

Then he remembered. Sara's train was an excursion, which meant it would probably follow this regular train and was still in the station.

Outside now he heard: "*All aboard.*"

He dashed for the vestibule.

The train began to move. It picked up speed. He stood there with his heart pounding and his skin crawling while New York vanished. His legs felt wobbly and all hollow when he finally stumbled back inside Old-Timer and collapsed on the nearest seat.

He was headed for Washington. Alone. And he had this sack of money he didn't know what to do with. The world was zipping by a mile a minute and his head felt as if it were whirling on a nonstop merry-go-round.

Was this really happening to him, Lincoln Farnum? Maybe he was imagining it all. Maybe his imagination had got stuck, like a needle on a phonograph record, and couldn't get unstuck, and he was really back home in the apartment and his school bag was filled with books and peanut-butter sandwiches. He opened it and looked. It was still money. Reaching in, he took out one of the stacks and examined a bill. Abraham Lincoln's picture was on it. THE UNITED STATES OF AMERICA, WASHINGTON, D.C., he read.

That made him feel better. Mr. Lincoln was his special friend, and the money was headed back in the direction from which it had come in the first place. In a way, it was as if he were on official business for Mr. Lincoln. And besides, Sara was on a train right behind this one. He'd wait for her in the Washington station, and when she learned about the money she would know at once what to do.

As he slipped the money back into the bag, Lincoln noticed the man sitting across the aisle. He was reading a newspaper and he was wearing black glasses. Lincoln's favorite television show was *The Spy in the Sky*. The spy traveled by airplane and he always wore black glasses. Now the man looked up from his newspaper and stared straight across the aisle at Lincoln. Lincoln couldn't see the man's eyes because of the glasses, but on television when the spy took his glasses off his eyes were dark and piercing. Actually, they were X-ray eyes that looked straight through his victim and read his thought.

Quick as a flash, Lincoln looked away and dropped the bag of money to the floor and planted his feet firmly on it.

He was a special courier in Mr. Lincoln's army and he had this dispatch case filled with valuable papers to deliver to Mr. Lincoln in Washington. The enemy was all around, plotting to get the papers. Lincoln bent over, to make sure the papers hadn't disappeared from under his feet, just as a pair of black shoes advanced along the aisle and halted alongside the dispatch case.

The shoes were attached to legs in uniform. Lincoln thought about drawing his rifle and rattling his saber, but he couldn't move, he was frozen scared, bent over like a pretzel.

A voice roared above him: "TICKET PLEASE!"

Ticket?

Lincoln's head snapped up like a jack-in-the-box. Would they put him off the train? Take him to jail? He blinked and looked up into the pink face of the conductor; he swallowed, trying to unstick his voice.

"Where are your folks, boy?" the conductor prodded. "Do they have your ticket?"

Lincoln shook his head.

The man in the dark glasses leaned across the aisle and laughed. "Maybe you've got another runaway, John."

The conductor pursed his lips and raised his eyebrows. "So you've got no ticket and no folks?"

Lincoln's voice came back in a rush. "I have too got folks—Mom and Pop, and there's Sissy and Sassy, and Herman-to-be, and I'm going to meet my sister Sara in Washington, and I've got money to pay my fare."

"Well then," the conductor said. "I'll have five dollars and thirty-three cents, please."

Lincoln reached into his pockets and counted out the money.

"I should charge you ten cents extra for not having a

ticket," the conductor said. "Buy yourself a coke—the railroad's treat."

Lincoln grinned and thanked the nice conductor.

The man in the black glasses reached across the aisle and handed Lincoln a package of gum. He took off his glasses. His eyes were blue and friendly. He wasn't a spy after all.

Lincoln was just a little disappointed at this. But then he took his feet off the military secrets and began to enjoy his adventure. Imagine him, Lincoln Farnum, headed for Washington, and his sister Sara on a train right behind him not knowing a thing about it.

Pop called his train "my home on wheels," and Lincoln thought how cozy it was sitting here in Old-Timer as it clickety-clacked through new and exciting scenes.

When the sandwich man came through the car, Lincoln bought two hot dogs, a coke, and some candy.

This surely was more exciting than running through the apartment pretending he was on a train. This was real. He hummed to the "clickety-clack" tune of the rails. Later it changed to "clack-clack CLACK." Old-Timer had what Pop called "flat feet." One of its wheels was giving up. Maybe they'd be late getting in.

They were.

Already the sky was darkening. Why, Washington was a big city. Lincoln always thought of New York as giant and every other place as little.

He got goose bumps. His mouth went dry.

What was he worried about? Sara was following close behind.

When the train pulled into the station he was the first one off. He ran all the way to the inside and asked a trainman at which gate the excursion would come in.

"No more excursions tonight," the man told him. "There was one in about half an hour ago."

Sara's train had left ahead of the regular, not after. He had been stupid not to think of that. He'd never find her tonight.

Now what would he do?

Where should he go? Where could he sleep?

Lincoln was scared.

How much of his fifteen dollars did he have left? He dug into his pockets. He counted. He had exactly eight dollars and sixty-seven cents. *Money!* In his rush to get off the train and look for Sara, Lincoln had forgotten the bag. He had left Mr. Lincoln's bills back there in Old-Timer.

Lincoln raced back to the train.

It was still standing in the same place, but now it was empty. He ran straight to Old-Timer and dashed for his seat. The canvas bag was exactly as he had left it.

Just as he reached down to grasp it, the train gave a sharp jerk. Lincoln went sprawling into the aisle.

He scrambled to his feet.

The train was moving.

Bump! Bump! STOP.

Lincoln spun around like a top and landed across a seat.

"Ding! Ding!" Now they were going backwards.

B U M P!

The engine was switching, getting rid of its tail of cars. Soon Old-Timer was the only one left.

Ding Ding! Old-Timer was backed into a barnlike place.

BUMP! The engine went off by itself, leaving Old-Timer and Lincoln alone.

Men in overalls came and stood around the coach. Lincoln shrank back into his seat, but the men didn't look up into the windows. They looked down at the wheels. They crawled under Old-Timer.

BANG! Lincoln shot up a foot. He peeked out the window. Some of the men carried flashlights. They were working on Old-Timer's flat feet with hammers and torches and wrenches.

The men talked and laughed while they worked. They were railroad men. Pop was a railroad man. As Lincoln listened to their voices he began to get drowsy. Pop said there was no better place to sleep than on a train. Lincoln made a pillow out of the bag of money and closed his eyes.

When he opened them it was light. Watery light.

Swish! Swish! Swish!

What was that? He sat bolt upright. He was under water but he wasn't wet. Where was he?

He came fully awake. He was in Old-Timer. A mop appeared at the window. Old-Timer was getting a bath. Next the cleaners would probably come into the coach. He had to get out. It was morning in Washington and he must find Sara.

Lincoln slung the bag of money over his shoulder and, when no one was looking, hopped off the coach and headed for the station, where he washed up extra clean in the rest room. Sara would throw a fit if he didn't look right.

Then he went into the coffee shop and bought himself a good breakfast—a hamburger and a milk shake. Now he felt ready for anything. Why, he'd find Sara without any trouble. She had said her group would probably go to the White House first thing. She'd be gawking at the sights and he'd bump smack into her. She'd tell him what to do about the money, and then after that he'd walk right into the White House and up the stairs to Mr. Lincoln's bedroom, and then after that he'd see the Lincoln Memorial and after that he'd have to catch the train in order to get home before Mrs. Readywell arrived to take care of him.

But first he had to find the White House.

Pop always said only two kinds of people were worth asking how to get places: taxi drivers and policemen.

There were no taxis about when Lincoln came out of the station, but he did see a long black car with a chauffeur standing alongside, so he walked right up and asked for directions.

The chauffeur grinned and pointed. "Right over there in front of the station you can get on a bus marked FRIENDSHIP HEIGHTS. You just missed one."

A man carrying a briefcase came hurrying.

"Good morning, Senator," the chauffeur said, opening the car door.

Then the chauffeur turned back to Lincoln. "There'll be another bus soon. It isn't very far to the White House."

The Senator leaned out the door. "I'm going to see the President. The boy can ride with us."

And so Lincoln stepped into the shiny black limousine and sat down right next to the Senator.

And that's how Lincoln went to the White House.

Things happened to Lincoln that never happened to

anyone else. If he told Sissy and Sassy that he saw Washington from a magic pumpkin, all painted shiny black, they'd laugh their heads off.

The Senator was very smart. Without asking any questions, he guessed right away that Lincoln had never before been to Washington. He pointed out the Capitol Building standing strong and high on the Hill. He asked the chauffeur to swing around so Lincoln could see the Washington Monument, and the Lincoln Memorial, grave and thoughtful in the distance.

Lincoln looked left and right trying to see all the famous places.

And then they were at the White House.

After he said good-bye to the Senator and to the chauffeur, Lincoln just stood there looking at his White House. He peered through the high gates and he saw that his house was shining white and stood in a green park with singing fountains. Bright flowers lined the walks, and trees shaded the grass. Lincoln felt so proud of his house he got a funny feeling in his chest like when he saw the Stars and Stripes go by in a parade.

Already a line had begun to form. Lincoln walked up and down the sidewalk looking for Sara. He realized that finding her wasn't going to be so easy. There were crowds of children and teen-agers. Groups of grown-ups. People dressed in their church clothes, and others who looked as if they were camping, came walking, or in cars, or in taxis. The cars had license plates from states far and near.

The visitors had all kinds of voices—soft-as-velvet kind, and the kind that twanged like Uncle Jay's guitar. There were slow and careful voices, as if the words were still new to the speakers and each one must be thought about separately.

A column of Boy Scouts came marching—hip—hip—hip. Lincoln got in line right behind them.

A band played in the distance. Three airplanes roared overhead. A high school group poured out of a bus. The boys wore beanies with WASHINGTON on them, and the girls wore head scarves decorated with Washington scenes. This reminded Lincoln to look for Sara. But he couldn't leave the line or he'd lose his place.

"We're moving," someone shouted, and the line hushed and went forward through the tall gates, past the guards, and up the curving walk.

When Lincoln walked through the big doors of the White House he had the feeling that his feet were not touching the pavement and his head was a balloon floating in midair.

At home, Lincoln had a tube-shaped toy called a kaleidoscope that held loose bits of colored glass. When he looked through one end of it, the glass pieces reflected against mirrors and made pretty patterns. Now Lincoln felt as if he were in a giant kaleidoscope as he walked through the beautiful rooms. Color patterns kept exploding at each turning. The colors went from gold to green to blue to red.

The patterns formed chandeliers of diamonds, floors like mirrors, candles and flowers. There were square rooms, oval rooms, velvets and satins. Paintings of past Presidents and First Ladies. Benjamin Franklin's picture, all life and color, was in the Green Room; the bare floor of the Blue Room was polished to a high shine and made Lincoln's feet itch to do a jig, but he'd never sit on Dolly Madison's sofa in the Red Room. It was for storybook ladies in rustly silks and laces. There was so much to see so swiftly. Lincoln tried to make memories of the patterns before each new burst of color.

The dining room, all white and gold, was so big Lincoln thought that even if all his relations came to dinner they wouldn't half fill it.

But the best was yet to come. All of this was leading up to the moment when he would see his bedroom.

The line moved out into the wide, red-carpeted hall. Now Lincoln saw that the great stairway leading to the next floor was roped off, and the line was moving toward the outside. He hesitated. A guard motioned him on. "But we didn't see Lincoln's bedroom," Lincoln said.

"We have about ten thousand visitors, and just two hours' time," the guard said.

"But my name is Lincoln, and I came all the way from New York."

"Some of these tourists are from Alaska and California and foreign lands," the guard said. "Here, you can have this guidebook. It has a nice picture of Lincoln's bedroom."

Lincoln thanked the guard and followed the crowd outside and through the gates. He stood looking back at his White House. He had not seen his bedroom. He had not found Sara.

Now the pack on his back felt heavy.

He had been foolish to think he would find Sara in such a big city. She had said that Washington belonged to the people. They were surely taking it over; crowds pressing into this place and that. Time was pressing, too. He had very little of it left before he must be on a train going home. But he couldn't leave without trying to see the Lincoln Memorial. It would probably be like Lincoln's bedroom; he wouldn't get anywhere near it.

And then he'd have to go straight to the police station. It was what he should have been smart enough to do in the first place. They would ask him all kinds of questions; they'd hold him, maybe in a jail cell; they'd call Pop.

Lincoln started walking. He thought about how he had not performed as Pop would like, as an engineer who knew where he was going and how to get there.

Pop called the caboose on his train "the Clown Wagon." Lincoln guessed that was where he really belonged—in the Clown Wagon.

He felt ashamed. Sissy and Sassy would never stop laughing. "Imagine Lincoln taking a sack of money from a stranger and really believing it was sandwiches," they would say.

Sara would be impatient. "Imagine Lincoln following me all the way to Washington . . ."

And poor Pop, who taught his family to do right, would look as if he'd allowed Lincoln to run wild, like a handcar going downhill without brakes.

Aunt Charlotte would have a good faint, and Uncle Jay would ask how he expected to be a top basketball player if he didn't use his head.

And Herman . . . Lincoln didn't want Herman ever to find out he had such a stupid brother. Maybe it would be just as well if the baby turned out to be a Hermione.

And then Lincoln reached the Lincoln Memorial.

When he looked up into the face of the great figure,

he knew all at once that the President had been waiting for him, for he sat relaxed in his chair, his expression kindly, unhurried.

In all of busy, crowded Washington, the President had time. Lincoln told him about his troubles, silently of course, and the President listened most attentively. In the misty light about his face, his lips seemed to move in answer. "You have been brave to come such a long way alone, Lincoln Farnum, and I thank you."

Courier Lincoln Farnum of the Union Army stood proudly and saluted his Commander in Chief.

And now, across the Courier's vision, strode a man wearing black glasses.

A spy!

"The papers," Lincoln seemed to say, his arms outstretched.

In one quick movement, Courier Lincoln Farnum slid the bag with its military secrets from his shoulder. He tossed it high—a perfect arc—like Uncle Jay's championship shot. It came to rest at the President's feet.

And then, before the onlookers grasped what had happened, Lincoln ran down into the crowd. He stood there grinning as people shouted and pointed to the sack, and guards swarmed about.

And then, for goodness sakes, if he didn't see Sara. She was with her class, walking toward the monument, so close to Lincoln he could have reached out and touched her. Instead, he ducked. He had taken care of matters himself.

Who was in charge of Lincoln?

Lincoln.

One day he would come back to Washington, when he was big so he wouldn't have to worry about grown-ups worrying about him. He would stay as long a time as he needed to see everything—the Eternal Flame—the Pentagon—the Senate in session. But now he must go home.

THE CRICKET IN TIMES SQUARE

by George Selden

Mario was alone in the subway station at Times Square. Every Saturday night for almost a year he had tended his father's newsstand. It was late. The station was empty, waiting for the crowds that never came. Tucker, a mouse, watched the boy.

Mario heard the sound too. He stood up and listened intently. The noise of the shuttle rattled off into silence. From the streets above came the quiet murmur of the late traffic. There was a noise of rustling nothingness in the station. Still Mario listened, straining to catch the mysterious sound. . . . And there it came again.

It was like a quick stroke across the strings of a violin, or like a harp that had been plucked suddenly. If a leaf in a green forest far from New York had fallen at midnight through the darkness into a thicket, it might have sounded like that.

Mario thought he knew what it was. The summer before he had gone to visit a friend who lived on Long Island. One afternoon, as the low sun reached long yellow fingers through the tall grass, he had stopped beside a meadow to listen to just such a noise. But there had been many of them then—a chorus. Now there was only one. Faintly it came again through the subway station.

Mario slipped out of the newsstand and stood waiting. The next time he heard the sound, he went toward it. It seemed to come from one corner, next to the stairs that led up to Forty-second Street. Softly Mario went toward the spot. For several minutes there was only the whispering silence. Whatever it was that was making the sound had heard him coming and was quiet. Silently Mario waited. Then he heard it again, rising from a pile of waste papers and soot that had blown against the concrete wall.

He went down and very gently began to lift off the

papers. One by one he inspected them and laid them to one side. Down near the bottom the papers became dirtier and dirtier. Mario reached the floor. He began to feel with his hands through the dust and soot. And wedged in a crack under all the refuse, he found what he'd been looking for.

It was a little insect, about an inch long and covered with dirt. It had six legs, two long antennae on its head and what seemed to be a pair of wings folded on its back. Holding his discovery as carefully as his fingers could, Mario lifted the insect up and rested him in the palm of his hand.

"A cricket!" he exclaimed.

Keeping his cupped hand very steady, Mario walked back to the newsstand. The cricket didn't move. And he didn't make that little musical noise any more. He just lay perfectly still—as if he were sleeping, or frightened to death.

Mario pulled out a tissue of Kleenex and laid the cricket on it. Then he took another and started to dust him off. Ever so softly he tapped the hard black shell, and the antennae, and legs, and wings. Gradually, the dirt that had collected on the insect fell away. His true color was still black, but now it had a bright glossy sheen.

When Mario had cleaned off the cricket as much as he could, he hunted around the floor of the station for a matchbox. In a minute he'd found one and knocked out one end. Then he folded a sheet of Kleenex, tucked it in the box and put the cricket in. It made a perfect bed. The cricket seemed to like his new home. He moved around a few times and settled himself comfortably.

Mario sat for a time, just looking. He was so happy and excited that when anyone walked through the station, he forgot to shout "Newspapers!" and "Magazines!"

Then a thought occurred to him: perhaps the cricket was hungry. He rummaged through his jacket pocket and found a piece of chocolate bar that had been left over from supper. Mario broke off one corner and held it out to the cricket on the end of his finger. Cautiously the insect lifted his head to the chocolate. He seemed to smell it a moment, then took a bite. A shiver of pleasure went over Mario as the cricket ate from his hand.

Mama and Papa Bellini came up the stairs from the lower level of the station. Mama was a short woman—a little stouter than she liked to admit—who wheezed and got a red face when she had to climb steps. Papa was tall and somewhat bent over, but he had a kindness that shone about him. There seemed always to be something smiling inside Papa. Mario was so busy feeding his cricket that he didn't see them when they came up to the newsstand.

"So?" said Mama, craning over the counter. "What now?"

"I found a cricket!" Mario exclaimed. He picked the insect up very gently between his thumb and forefinger and held him out for his parents to see.

Mama studied the little black creature carefully. "It's a bug," she pronounced finally. "Throw it away."

Mario's happiness fell in ruins. "No, Mama," he said anxiously. "It's a special kind of bug. Crickets are good luck."

"Good luck, ay?" Mama's voice had a way of sounding very dry when she didn't believe something. "Cricketers are good luck—so I suppose ants are better luck. And cockroaches are the best luck of all. Throw it away."

"Please, Mama, I want to keep him for a pet."

"No bugs are coming to my house," said Mama. "We've got enough already with the screens full of holes. He'll whistle to his friends—they'll come from all over—we'll have a houseful of cricketers."

"No we won't," said Mario in a low voice. "I'll fix the screens." But he knew it was no use arguing with Mama. When she had made up her mind, you might as well try to reason with the Eighth Avenue subway.

"How was selling tonight?" asked Papa. He was a peaceful man and always tried to head off arguments. Changing the subject was something he did very well.

"Fifteen papers and four magazines," said Mario. "And Paul just bought a Sunday *Times*."

"No one took a *Musical America*, or anything else nice?" Papa was very proud that his newsstand carried all of what he called the "quality magazines."

"No," answered Mario.

"So you spend less time playing with cricketers, you'll sell more papers," said Mama.

"Oh now, now," Papa soothed her. "Mario couldn't help it if nobody buys."

"You can tell the temperature with crickets too," said Mario. "You count the number of chirps in a minute, divide by four and add forty. They're very intelligent."

"Who needs a cricketer-thermometer?" said Mama. "It's coming on summer, it's New York—it's hot. And how do you know so much about cricketers. Are you one?"

"Jimmy Lebovski told me last summer," said Mario.

"Then give it to the expert Jimmy Lebovski," said Mama. "Bugs carry germs. He doesn't come in the house."

Mario looked down at his new friend in the palm of his hand. Just for once he had been really happy. The cricket seemed to know that something was wrong. He jumped onto the shelf and crept into the matchbox.

"He could keep it here in the newsstand," suggested Papa.

Mario jumped at that idea. "Yes, and then he wouldn't have to come home. I could feed him here, and leave him here, and you'd never have to see him," he said to Mama. "And when you took the stand, I'd bring him with me."

Mama paused. "Cricketer," she said scornfully. "What do we want with a cricketer?"

"What do we want with a newsstand?" said Papa. "We got it—let's keep it." There was something resigned, but nice, about Papa.

"You said I could have a dog," said Mario, "but I never got him. And I never got a cat, or a bird, or anything. I wanted this cricket for my pet."

"He's yours then," said Papa. And when Papa spoke in a certain quiet tone—that was all there was to it. Even Mama didn't dare disagree.

She took a deep breath. "Oh well—" she sighed. And Mario knew it would be all right. Mama's saying "oh well" was her way of giving in. "But only on trial he stays. At the first sign of the cricketer friends, or if we come down with peculiar diseases—out he goes!"

"Yes, Mama, anything you say," said Mario.

"Come on, Mario," Papa said. "Help me close up."

Mario held the matchbox up to his eye. He was sure the cricket looked much happier, now that he could stay. "Goodnight," he said. "I'll be back in the morning."

"Talking to it yet!" said Mama. "I've got a cricketer for a son."

Papa took one side of the cover to the newsstand, Mario the other, and together they fitted it on. Papa locked it down. As they were going downstairs to the trains, Mario looked back over his shoulder. He could almost feel the cricket, snugged away in his matchbox bed, in the darkness.

MAPLE STREET

by Nan Hayden Agle

Margaret Gage, a nine-year-old black girl, was sitting
alone on the white marble steps of 914 Maple Street.
She had been there since early morning, watching the
movers bring furniture out of the house next door and
load it into the moving van parked at the curb.

It hurt to see the familiar couch carried down the
steps, and when the mahogany living room table came
through the door she turned her head away.

This was just about the worst day of Margaret's life.

It *was* the worst. The Kemps were moving away and Betty Kemp was her best friend. She and Betty had grown up together. They had played together every day, checkers on that table, guessing games on that couch.

Betty was great at pretending. Tell her you had on a mink coat and she'd say, "It looks grand on you, Margaret, and your feather hat and high-heel pumps are perfect with it," when you really had on a plaid shift, no hat, and loafers. She and Margaret would giggle and giggle over nothing at all. Papa said he'd never known any two people to have more fun. And now Betty was moving away.

No more playing together. No more racing down Maple Street to see who could get to the mailbox first. Maple Street was only one block long, row houses—903 to 928. You could see the numbers flash by as you ran fast.

There were other girls on Maple Street and loads of boys but Margaret knew not one of them could ever take Betty's place.

Around two o'clock in the afternoon the loaded van pulled away from the curb and went up the street. Before it turned the corner Betty came out of her house lugging a suitcase in one hand and a bulging shopping bag in the other. She had on two hats, her Sunday straw on top of the old green beanie, enough to make you die laughing any other day.

"We're about to leave now, Margaret," Betty said, tilting her head to keep from losing the hats. Seeing her friend's soft mouth down at the corners, she added, "Don't feel too sad. You'll be moving soon yourself. All of the best people are moving up town."

"No, they aren't," declared Margaret, part of her sorrow switching quickly to anger. "Mama and Papa and Granpa and I are not moving."

She stood up, tossed her shoulder-length braids back and said, "Even if we wanted to move, which we don't, we wouldn't on account of Granpa."

"I know your grandfather does real good, Margaret, everybody thinks so," Betty told her. "But my mother says she's surprised you've stayed here this long, your father being a school principal and all."

"Maple Street is a good place to live no matter what you do or who you are," Margaret said. "It is one of the best streets in Baltimore!"

Betty set the suitcase and the bag down on the pavement. She shrugged her shoulders and the hats tilted over her eyes as she said, "Maybe it was once, before those vacant lots at the corner got to be such a mess."

"The rest is okay," put in Margaret.

"No, it's going downhill fast," Betty answered. "My

mother says it started downhill the day Mr. Hubner bought 922 and made it into apartments. She says people who rent apartments to other people don't take care of their property the way owners who live there do."

"Some don't, some do."

"Well, Mr. Hubner is a don't, so *I* hear," Betty told Margaret. Then, giving her a friendly shove, she added, "You'll *die*, positively die when you hear this. He bought our house."

"Oh, Betty, no!"

"Mother's motioning to me, I've got to go."

Betty hugged Margaret, pushed the hats in place again and said, "We'll still be best friends, won't we, no matter how far apart we are?"

Margaret nodded. She watched Betty get into the blue car with her mother and drive away. Just before the car turned the corner Betty leaned out the window and waved, and Margaret burst into tears.

The tears were partly because Betty had gone, partly because Betty had said Maple Street was going down-hill, and partly because she felt guilty.

Today was a school day, Friday, end of the first week of June, and Margaret had stayed home to be near Betty till the very last. She'd pretended she had a sore throat. That kind of pretending was dishonest, she knew it was. Still she'd said she had a sore throat and Mama believed her and let her stay home.

She hoped Papa wouldn't find out she'd fibbed. He would be angry with her, real angry. She hoped Granpa wouldn't find out either because he would be sorry.

Granpa was coming now. She could hear his footsteps in the hall.

"Here, child, sweep," Granpa said, stepping carefully over the doorsill, the red-handled broom in his hand. "I heard you crying, saying good-by to your friend. Your grandmother used to sweep when she had a sorrow. She didn't sweep it away, nothing will do that, but somehow sweeping helped. Give it a try."

Granpa Pinkney was eighty years old, a lean, slightly built man. He was darker than Margaret and much darker than Mama. He held his shoulders back and his head high so his dark glasses wouldn't slip down his blunt nose and let people see blind eyes.

"Here, honey. Take the broom."

Margaret hugged him, and the broom clattered down the steps, landing slap on the sidewalk. She loved Granpa dearly. Mama and Papa did, too.

Granpa had started to work as a carpenter when he was fourteen and worked until he went blind ten years ago. He and Granma, dead a long time now, had five children—three girls and two boys—and they sent every one of them through college. Mama, the youngest, and two of the others were teachers. Her oldest sister, a graduate nurse, was supervisor in a hospital in New Jersey, and one brother was a chemist in Boston.

Everybody on Maple Street respected Granpa. "Good evening, Mr. Pinkney. How are you today?" they'd say as they passed the house, Granpa sitting on the steps. Even grouchy, deaf old Mrs. Carter who lived across the street had a good word for Granpa and she didn't for anybody else. Papa said she was grouchy because she didn't want to be on welfare. She had to be, though, as the rent Mr. Ritter paid her for one room wasn't enough to live on.

Margaret picked up the broom. Sweep, sweep, sweep —she swept vigorously, thinking about Maple Street, not Betty. Nobody else was on welfare except the Murdocks who lived on the first floor at 922, and they were coming off as soon as Mrs. Murdock learned to sew.

Mama said Mrs. Murdock was a fine person, reliable and trustworthy. Her husband wasn't, which was why his family was on welfare. He ran off with the alto at the Baptist Church on the corner, left no money and two children—Ursula, a stylish-looking eighteen-year-old girl, a senior in high school, and Feemster, a thirteen-year-old boy. Ursula wasn't a bit of trouble but

Feemster was. Ask anybody. First thing people said when the news got out about Mr. Murdock and the alto was, "Poor Mrs. Murdock, with that boy to look after!"

Sometimes Margaret couldn't stand Feemster Murdock. Just thinking about him made her sweep faster. He teased her something awful, called her stuck up because she went to a private school and the Episcopal Church. Well, she did go to Friends School, the best school in Baltimore or any place else, Papa said. She had started there in the nursery school when she was four years old. Most of the children at Friends were white. Not all though; at the last assembly Margaret had counted twenty-three black faces, not including her own.

There wasn't much dirt to sweep into the gutter in front of Footners' and Greens' as Mrs. Footner and Mrs. Green were excellent housekeepers. However, in front of Mr. Percy Weldon's house, last one up, there was plenty. No scraps of paper or cigar butts or anything like that, just a normal amount of everyday dirt and dust a bachelor like Mr. Weldon wouldn't even notice. Margaret swept up a good pile, then swished it out into the street.

She swept on to the corner, stopped, and frowned at the vacant lots—904 and 906.

What a mess!

The houses had been knocked down and hauled away several years before when a supermarket was supposed to be built there. For some reason it never was. In time the lots were bought for a new school but that had also fallen through—too close to 61, Mama's school, so people said. After that nothing happened.

Children played on the lots and people, not Maple Streeters, dumped things there: old washing machines, refrigerators, bedsprings—big things the garbage man wouldn't take. The boys in the neighborhood built a splendid clubhouse out of the junk—roof, floor, windows, and all. It was fun but didn't last very long. Boys from another neighborhood knocked it down and one of them cut his toe kicking in the door, cut it so badly he had to go to the hospital and have it sewed up.

After that the Civic League or some group like that made the city put a fence around the lots so children couldn't get hurt and hopefully to keep people from dumping more junk there. Officer Pike put up KEEP OFF signs on all four sides.

Margaret liked Officer Pike. Everybody who kept the law did. He was big and handsome with broad shoulders, and real strong. His face was strong, too. Seeing it, you minded what he said.

Margaret leaned the broom against the fence and looked through the wire mesh.

No wonder Betty said Maple Street was going downhill. Look at all those broken-up boxes, old rags, that frayed oily rope, a chair with no legs, the boys' club-house bashed in and toppled over, worn-out tires, a rusty bedspring, an old ripped shirt, a faded soggy gray blanket that once was pink.

Right in the middle of everything ugly there was something green growing. Margaret couldn't make out what it was. A heavy tire was leaning against it, and it blocked her view.

Margaret loved anything that had roots in the earth. She stooped to try to get a better look, then went around the corner to see if she could see it from that side.

It was a little tree, about as tall as she was, maybe not quite as tall. Bent over, it was hard to tell for sure. Two of its five branches stuck straight up in the air. One nearly touched the ground, and still another reached out to her almost like an arm.

The tree was extra pretty in the middle of all the ugly junk. But how sad it looked, all bent over. Every living thing wanted to grow straight, Margaret thought. Well, not vines and some squatty bushes, but most every thing. For sure this tree wanted to.

She had to do something about it.

If only she could push the tire out of the way, the tree would spring straight. She ran to the corner, the Maple Street corner, picked up the broom and ran back with it. Stooping, her full short skirt fanning out like a lamp shade, she poked the handle of the broom through the wire. It was not quite long enough.

"My, my, what is Miss Gage up to?" asked a familiar voice behind her. It was Feemster Murdock on his way home from school.

Margaret ignored the teasing "Miss Gage" and said over her shoulder, "I'm trying to rescue that little tree, trying to push the tire away from it, but I can't reach far enough. See if you can, Feemie, please?"

Bang! A stack of books landed on the pavement, Modern Math flopping open on top of English Composition.

Feemster bent down, put his hands on his knees, and inspected the tree. He was a short boy with large feet and hands. Seeing him, you were sure he'd be big some day if he lived long enough. He was in Mama's class at School 61 and she said she didn't for the life of her see how he had made it to the sixth grade as he couldn't read a stop sign without the red and green lights to give him a hint.

Smart, though. Feemster Murdock was smart, no doubt about that. He just couldn't or wouldn't read. Mrs. Murdock was helping him with his lessons at night and sometimes Mama tutored him holidays. His mother declared he was going to graduate from high school if it took him twenty years, and at the rate he was going it might.

"The poor itty-bitty thing, all bent over," Feemster said, pretending to be upset about the tree. "Ain't it a shame? I'm going to cry. Boo-hoo."

Margaret was so mad she rushed at him. He dodged, yelling "Help, help, save me!" and grinned like anything. Then he wiped the grin off with his hand, a habit he had. Looking serious now, forehead wrinkled, he said, "Before I do any boy scouting for you, Miss Gage, what kind of a tree is this you are so anxious to rescue?"

"I don't know, Feemie."

"Then the deal is off. No, wait. Here comes Mr. Avery. He'll know. He knows everything, so he says."

Mr. Quillen Avery, Maple Street 917, was a distinguished-looking gentleman from the West Indies. He had midnight-black skin and straight black hair which he kept trimmed and well oiled at all times. He wore expensive suits of top quality, well cut. People said he had some sort of secret job with the government, but nobody knew for sure what he did. He owned a Cadillac, two Siamese cats, a color television set, and he had a housekeeper, Mrs. Urf. He often went on trips, taking the Cadillac with him and leaving the cats with Mrs. Urf.

"Good afternoon, Mr. Avery," Feemster said extra-politely as though he were the best boy in the country. "Would you be kind enough to tell us what kind of a tree this is?"

Mr. Avery approached, taking long unhurried strides somewhat like those of Officer Pike. He studied the little tree through the wire, cleared his throat, said one word, "Peach," and left at the same measured pace.

"A peach tree. Isn't that wonderful?" Margaret said, delighted over the news. "Just think, somebody ate a peach, tossed the seed over the fence or maybe tossed it onto the vacant lot before the fence was up, and it grew. Isn't that wonderful, Feemie?"

"Spare me the hearts and flowers nature study lesson and get out of the way," he said, flinging both arms out. "Feemster Murdock is about to go into action."

He flopped on the pavement and with legs spread wide he poked the handle of the broom through the fence as far as it would go.

"I can't reach it either. I give up." He rolled over on his back and lay there, eyes closed, the broom a lily on his chest.

"Oh!" Margaret felt terribly discouraged.

Feemster opened his eyes, looked up at her, and said, "I'll boost you over the fence and you can save the poor teenie-weenie peach tree yourself."

"I'd be scared," Margaret said, backing away.

Feemster sprang to his feet, saying, "Okay. Let the stupid tree stay bent or die. I don't care."

As he bent over to pick up his books Margaret had to do something. She couldn't just let him go. Grabbing the broom, she gave him a swift whack across the seat.

Feemster staggered and collapsed, putting on a big act as he yelled, "Help, police!"

"Be quiet," Margaret hissed at him. "You'll wake up Mr. Weldon." Mr. Weldon was the night watchman at the nut and bolt factory and he slept in the daytime.

Too late. Mr. Weldon's pinched brown face full of worry lines appeared at the second floor side window of 908 and he called out in an irritated voice, "What's going on down there?"

"I'm terribly sorry, Mr. Weldon. It was all my fault," Margaret explained.

The window banged shut.

"I don't blame him a bit for being mad, all that yelling when he was trying to sleep," Margaret said.

Feemie reached for his books once again and Margaret pulled at his arm saying, "Wait. See that hole down under the fence?"

"Where at?"

"There." Margaret pointed. "This side of the orange crate just beyond that hunk of rug or whatever it is."

"Yea," Feemie said. "Some dog, the Bookers' dog I guess, dug it trying to get inside the fence to catch rats. So it's a hole under the fence, so what?"

"If you'd dig it a little bit deeper and wider and at the same time bend up the wire some, I might be able to squeeze under. I'm a pretty good squeezer," Margaret told him.

Feemster's eyebrows went up a notch and his eyes took on a shocked expression. "You, Miss Gage, of all people, contributing to the delinquency of a minor."

"What do you mean?"

"Just what I said. Here I am, an innocent young boy, and you ask me to tamper with somebody else's property. You suggest, no you urge me, to break the law."

Before Margaret could think of a thing to say he added crisply, "Hand me that piece of pipe laying there close to the fence."

Margaret reached through the wire and dragged out a short length of pipe rusty at one end. She handed it to Feemster, saying, "Here. Be quick before somebody comes. I'll keep watch."

While Feemster Murdock dug and dug and pried up on the stiff wire, Margaret looked up the street and down. When the hole was about three fourths deep enough she saw Clinton Short sauntering by on the other side. Clinton was fourteen, proper, took violin lessons, and was very studious but Feemie didn't hold that against him. In fact he and Clint were best friends.

"Hurry up," Margaret warned, "Clinton just passed going home from school. He didn't see us but somebody else might. Hurry!"

"Clinton?" Without saying another word to Margaret, Feemster dropped the pipe, leaped to his feet, and ran down Maple Street full tilt yelling, "Hey, Clint, wait for me!" loud enough to shatter Mr. Weldon's nerves.

Margaret called, "Feemie, come back," knowing perfectly well he wouldn't. If she were playing a game with somebody he'd hang around and hang around, but now when she needed him most he ran off. That was just exactly like him. Still he had done some digging, which was a help.

Margaret dug by herself for a few more minutes, then decided to give it a try. She lay flat on her stomach and inched under the wire, head low, pushing with elbows, knees, and toes. It wasn't easy to squeeze under, not a bit easy. Twice she got stuck and had to back out and start over.

On the third try, after losing one red hair ribbon, tearing the back of her blouse, and getting dirt all over the front of it, she made it.

Inside the fence now—good. Margaret knew she must be swift, rescue the peach tree, and get out before anybody saw her. Wait, there was the young Reverend Dawson walking on the other side of the street, taking quick, wide steps as though he had to save the whole world before sundown.

Margaret was sure he would approve of her helping the tree because he was all for helping everybody and everything that needed help. Still, like Papa, he was a stickler for keeping the law and he would not approve of anybody being inside a fence that had KEEP OUT signs on it. She ducked out of sight behind an ancient icebox with one door missing, the other door hanging by a single hinge.

As soon as the Reverend Dawson had gone on by she came out, snagged her left sock on an orange crate, jumped over a bashed-in breadbox, and there in reach at last was the peach tree. Close up it was even more pitiful than from far off. It really needed help.

Margaret tried to lift the tire, but couldn't—it was too heavy, and besides it was stuck in the ground. She leaned her shoulder against it and pushed with all her might. It didn't budge. She heaved up on it; still nothing happened. She tried pulling it, digging her heels in the earth. That didn't work either. She backed off and kicked it in six different places hard enough to hurt her toe. The last kick finally jarred the tire loose. Margaret rolled it away.

But the tree did not spring straight. She would have to tie it to a stick or something. Feemie's digging pipe would do fine, and luckily it was near enough to the fence for her to reach. She hammered it into the soft ground close to the tree with a brickbat she found right at her feet. Then she straightened the little tree and tied it to the pipe with a strip from a dirty old shirt that was lying under the edge of the orange crate.

Her work done, Margaret stood back and looked at the tree. In time it would stand straight by itself. She was pretty sure of that. Now she had better get out of the lot while her luck was still holding.

Squeezing out was not as easy as squeezing in, and squeezing in hadn't been easy. Margaret got stuck halfway through, good and stuck. She couldn't move an inch forward or back.

"Feemie!" she yelled hopefully. Maybe he would hear her and come to her rescue. He should have come back anyway; leaving her the way he had done wasn't fair and he knew it. "Feemie!"

Presently she heard footsteps—not Feemie's—heavy, measured, slow steps. She couldn't turn her head to see who was coming and she held her breath, hoping the steps would go the other way. Instead they came closer,

closer, and stopped right there in front of her nose which was practically on the ground.

Big shiny black shoes, blue pants. Margaret didn't dare look up, she was too scared.

The shoes stayed put and a deep, familiar voice said, "Margaret Gage, what are you doing under that fence?"

It was Officer Pike, looking enormous from her view as he stretched up, up to brass buttons and terribly official blue policeman's hat. She tried to speak but couldn't.

"Come out of there at once," he ordered. "You know very well you are breaking the law. Come on out."

"I'm trying to, Officer Pike. That's just what I am trying to do. But I'm stuck."

Instead of helping her he paced up and down and said, "I knew some child would get into trouble over this vacant lot, or hurt. However," he paused, "I did not expect it to be Margaret Gage."

Margaret wriggled, trying once more to free herself.

Finally Officer Pike stooped down, pulled her through, and set her on her feet, saying, "I was looking for Feemster Murdock. Have you seen him?"

"Feemster Murdock? What do you want him for?"

Margaret asked, smoothing down her short skirt and tucking in her blouse.

When Officer Pike said he'd found Feemster's books up at the corner and wanted to return them to him, she said, "Oh, is that all? I thought maybe he was in some sort of trouble."

"No, Margaret. You are."

"Don't tell on me, please, Officer Pike," Margaret begged. "You know how Papa is—and Mama and Granpa would be so hurt if they knew."

Officer Pike did not answer. He just looked down at Margaret.

She tilted her head to one side, looked up at him and said, "I am sorry."

"Sorry you got caught or sorry you broke the law?"

"Both. And yet I had to help the peach tree. I couldn't let it grow crooked forever. See," she pointed to the tree, "I tied it straight."

"You should have waited and asked me before you went inside the fence," Officer Pike said.

"I know, but I didn't. I wasn't thinking. Please promise not to tell on me."

Although Officer Pike made no promises, he smiled, which Margaret thought was a hopeful sign. Then they started down Maple Street.

As they walked along side by side Margaret told him

how Feemie had helped her get under the fence and how Betty had moved, which was very sad, and how Betty said Maple Street was going downhill.

"I wish it wouldn't," she said. "I want it to be the best street in the city."

Officer Pike said he did, too.

By that time they were near enough to 914 for Granpa to hear and recognize their footsteps.

"Good day, Officer Pike," Grandpa said. "And where have you been, young lady? You must have swept all the way to the harbor."

"The broom, I forgot the broom!" Margaret said and she ran back to the corner for it.

She got home in time to hear Officer Pike say, "Yes, Mr. Pinkney, your granddaughter and I both think the vacant lots are a blight on the neighborhood."

Granpa agreed and Margaret said, "What could we do? There must be something we could do about it."

As she spoke she beamed at Officer Pike, hoping he would know she was thanking him for not telling on her. He nodded his head ever so slightly, showing he had gotten the message. Then he left, saying he'd better get along to Murdocks' with Feemster's books.

In front of 916 he turned around and said to Granpa, "You know what I think, Mr. Pinkney? I think those lots would make a fine playground for the children of this neighborhood."

"Splendid," Granpa said, and Margaret exclaimed, "That's a *great* idea, simply great, Officer Pike!"

She could picture the whole thing—swings in the shade, seesaws, jungle gym, flowers along walks, green velvety grass, and in the middle of it all the little peach tree in bloom.

"How can we get it to be one?" she asked, jumping up and down, higher and higher until she was jumping higher than she'd ever jumped before.

Officer Pike said he didn't know. After some thought he added, "If I were you, Margaret, and I wanted that playground, I would write a letter to the mayor and ask *him* how to go about getting it."

"You would?" Margaret came to a fast stop.

"Yes," Officer Pike and Granpa said together.

Margaret thought a second before she said, "I'd write it now only Mama and Papa aren't home to help me and they won't be home until late. They are going to a school supper and a meeting."

"You don't need any help," Officer Pike told her. "Write it in your own words."

Then he walked on down Maple Street.

Granpa stayed there on the steps and Margaret went in the house and sat down at Papa's desk. She was pretty good in composition at school, got A on her report usually. But a letter to the mayor had to be A plus.

She pulled out the scratch pad, licked the end of the

pencil point, and wrote two sentences. They wouldn't do. She crumpled the page, dropped it into the wastebasket, and on a fresh sheet of paper wrote Dear Mayor and two more sentences, one of which was fairly good, though not nearly good enough. She threw that page away too and spread the third piece of paper in front of her, thinking hard.

"Granpa, are there two l's in marvelous?" she called out loud so he could hear.

ME AND ARCH AND THE PEST

by John Durham

Some folks say our dog's name is Ritter von Bulow the Third. And I guess that is his fancy name. That they put in the book, and all.

But Archie and me, we know his real name. It's Pest. We named him right and nobody else can tell us. Don't we feed him? Don't we walk him? Don't we brush him out and even cut his toenails? Didn't we save him from them dognappers? You bet we did.

Who else got a right to call what his name is? Especially some funny German name nobody understands.

I'll tell you how we got him, old Pest. And all the other things that happened. Archie and me was out this Saturday. Arch, he came by my house and yelled for me that mornin'.

Now me, I lived in this teensy little old house down in South L.A. That's almost in Watts, but not quite. It's a nice little old house. That got vines all over it, with these wild-looking purplish flowers. Only trouble is, South Los Angeles, it's mostly colored. Or my momma, she thinks it's trouble. She been moanin' about livin' in with the colored ever since we moved out from Georgia, three years ago.

But me, I like it. Heck, *Arch* is black. And me and Arch are just like *that*. Well, he's not black, actually. Actually, he's this nice smooth coffee color. Coffee with lots of cream. Only reason I mention it, is how my momma feels.

That mornin', I was back in the kitchen, having a little cornmeal mush and tea, like. When I heard old Arch first. Out front on the sidewalk.

"Bit!" old Archie called. I could hear him. From out on the sidewalk. "Hey, Bit! Come on out!"

"Who's that yellin'?" my momma, she called from the livin' room. "What's that awful noise out there?"

"I'm comin'," I yelled to Archie.

"You hear me, Bit?" my momma said. "Who is that? And stop that terrible screamin' in this house. You hear me?"

Momma, she's all right. She gets these sick headaches and this gastric distress, but she's nice, most of the time. It's just that she don't like the colored. You know. Hell, she grew up in Georgia. What you gonna do with a lady grew up in Georgia? Can't tell her nothin'. She won't even listen. So that morning I just sailed past her and out the screen door.

"You, there, Bit, you whoa!" she yelled.

But I was gone. Five minutes and she'd forget about it. I knew that.

"Hey, man!" Arch said, when I came out the door. "Whatcha doin', all that time? Huh?" He hit me on the shoulder. Kind of hard.

"Look out, man," I said. "You'll kill me with them powerful blows." I hit him back. Harder.

"You musta got stronger overnight," he said. "You couldn't hit like that yesterday."

"What's goin' on, dude?" I said.

He held up this old beat-up bat. "Let's hit a few," he said. "Over at Ella Wheeler Wilcox School."

"We can't do that, man," I said.

"Why's that?"

"With them powerful muscles of yours," I said, "you'll knock out picture windows a block away."

"We got to take the chance," he said. "The Dodgers need me."

"Oh," I said. "Yeah. I forgot about that. What's a few picture windows?"

We dogtrotted all the way, just to loosen up. We throw my ball back and forth as we go.

"Hey, man," I say, "how are things with us?"

"We all right, old buddy," Arch, he said. "Like that." He held up two fingers.

"How much bonus we gonna get?"

"A hundred thou apiece," he said. "Besides the two cars."

"What kinda cars they gonna be?"

"I thought a Lincoln Continental for starters. You know, for pickin' up the laundry. And maybe a Rolls-Royce for when I wants to put on the dog."

"I don't know," I said. "Maybe a Lincoln. But them Rolls. They just plain ugly to me."

"Your taste, it's all in your mouth," old Arch, he said. "Folks that know, they got Rollses."

"Folks that know," I said. We was joggin' along, like I say, and it come out like "Fo-holks tha-hat know." "Them folks bother me."

"Like what you mean?"

"Well," I said. "Like teachers, see?"

"Yeah," Arch said. "What about teachers?"

"Well," I said. "Teachers are supposed to know things. Right?"

"Right."

"But look at English teachers. They always tellin' you how to talk right. Right?"

"Man, they are."

"Like, you got to not say got. Right?"

"Right."

"But *folks*," I said. "They all say got. Like my poppa. Now, he says, 'I got no money.' But the English teacher, *she* say he can't say got. See what I mean?"

"Man, I know it. Way she says to talk, it don't feel natural. Your poppa, he a natural man."

"Right," I said. "He is *that*. So, how am I suppose to talk?"

"Me," Arch said, "I talk the way folks expect. You know?"

"What you mean?"

"Well, in English class, I talk the way the lady wants. But out here, where people is, I talk the way folks talk."

"I try to," I said. "I mean, I try to do that. But it mixes me up a little. Then, there's you black people."

"Yeah," Arch says. "There's us." He grins.

"Now you talk a little bitty bit different from my poppa. So me, I'm all mixed up, 'tween you and the teacher and my poppa."

"Thing to do," Arch said, "is to just open your mouth, baby, and let it roll out."

"Maybe," I said. "But then Old Lady Garrity, she wrinkles up her nose." Old Lady Garrity, she's my English teacher. "She makes faces when I just let it roll out."

"You want to be a natural man," Arch said, "you got to expect a little nose-wrinklin'."

"That is for dadgone sure," I said. The thing is, I want to be a natural man, all right. But I don't want folks like Old Lady Garrity makin' faces at me. I want her to smile when I talk. Because Old Lady Garrity, she's downright good-lookin'.

We got out on the grass playground at Ella Wheeler Wilcox. Arch, he's up first. He gets up there and I get way out. Because, man, he hits 'em. He whanged one out to me, way up there. Way up there against the smoggy blue. It was sailin' down to me, nice an easy. When something happened. I was reachin' up for it, you know, just like pickin' a raisin out of a fruitcake. When, Zip! Zap! Pow! Bang! Here comes this black and white streak. It sailed past my left shoulder and up and grabbed the ball.

"Watch out, man!" old Arch, he called. But too late. That big old dog *had* that ball. He caught it seven feet up. Neat and easy, he caught it. And he went loopin' on down that field. It took me a while to see him, he was goin' so fast. He run down past Arch and circled him. He come back and circled *me*. Just zippin'. He cut two figure eights like that. Then he stopped, just halfway between us. The ball was still in his mouth.

He looked at Arch, first. Then he looked at me. Then he dropped the ball on the grass. He put one big old paw on it. And he just looked at it.

Let me tell you about that dog. First off, he was big. I mean. You *think* big. But he was *big*. He was one of them police dogs, you know. A German shepherd, some calls 'em. His face, it was black, with little silvery white marks around the eyes. His tail and his legs, they was black, too. But all the rest of him was this kind of silvery white. You know? Like he been dusted with snow. He was a beauty, I tell you. But *big*.

"Look who got the ball," Arch said.

"You look."

"Who gonna get it?"

"You. If anybody does. Because I ain't."

"You chicken?" Arch said.

"You know it, man. I can cackle and I can crow. I might even lay you a egg or two."

"You think he's mean?" Arch said.

"Me, I'm not even gonna consider it," I said. "He's there and he's got my ball. He wants it that bad, he can have it."

"Ah, man, I just hit *one*."

"Hit away," I said. "I'm just the fielder."

"I think I gonna wait a while," Arch said. "He might get tired of standin' there."

"He don't look tired to me. Does he to you?"

"Not very." Arch, he sat down, holdin' the bat handy.

That big old dog, he looked at me. He looked at Arch. Then he barked.

"Sounds kind of playful," Arch said. "Don't it?"

"Maybe," I said. "You go play with him."

The dog, he picked up the ball in his mouth, then. He trotted toward me. Why pick on me? I thought. The dog come to within ten feet of me before he dropped the ball. He dropped it, then he looked up at me. He barked once. He barked twice.

"He wants to play," Arch said.

"Well, I don't," I said. "Leastways not with no monster like that."

The dog picked up the ball again. He come to within five feet of me and look like he was just comin' on *over* me. Then he dropped the ball again. And he looked up at me and *grinned.* Yeah. Just like a man. Like any human. And he barked twice.

"Oh, well," I said. "All right." Truth is, I was kind of tired of bein' chicken. He wasn't nothin' but a dog. I told myself that. So I went over and picked up the ball. Right out from under his nose. And I hauled back and threw it up to Arch.

That dog, I tell you. He got down there almost as fast as the ball. I never seen nothin' move no faster. He slid up to Arch like an old pro. Then he set there and watched while Arch threw the ball up and hauled back the bat to swing.

Arch connected, way he always does. And that dog was gone. He lit out. He was down there, settin', waitin' when that ball started down. I didn't even try to outfield him. Hell, I know when I'm beat. No human being ever caught a ball no neater, either. He caught it. And he brought it over to me and dropped it. Then he looked up at me and grinned.

"Smart alec," I said.

He barked, twice.

"Oh, all right," I said.

I picked up the ball and threw it down to Arch. This time I had more guts, when Arch hit a high one. I tried to beat out the dog. And I did. Course, he took the ball away from me. Soon as my feet hit the ground, he had it out my hand. And he trotted up to Arch and laid it in his hand. Then he waited, nice and polite, till Arch hit it down the field.

That went on for a hour. Till I was all tuckered out. I was draggin'.

"Hey, Arch," I yelled. "You field 'em for a while."

"No, man," he said.

"Well, then, let's quit." I looked at the dog. He was settin' there. Waitin' for Arch to hit another one. *He* wasn't tired, not one little bit. "You sure can break up a game," I said to him. "You're a pest, you know that?"

"Let's go down to the Taco Lita," Arch said. "I got some money."

"Okay," I said. We started off down the street. The dog, he just set there. Lookin' after us, like a man, his big old eyes bright. He just watched us.

"Bye-bye, pest," I said.

"He's a *dog*," Arch said, "that dog is." He looked back. "Look at 'im. He's a *dog*."

"He's a pest," I said. "You wasn't out there with him."

"He could take a man apart," Arch said.

"That's another thing tired me out," I said. "Just wonderin' if he was goin' to. You know?"

We didn't see him again. Not till the tacos was ready and I had mine raised up for the first bite. Then there he was. Settin' there in front of me. Grinnin'. And lookin' hungry.

"Aw, come on," I said to him. "Pester Arch this time."

"Here, dog," Arch said. "I ain't a stinge. I give you one of my tacos." And he threw him one.

"Looks like we got us a dog," Arch said.

"You," I said. "You got *you* a dog. Cost twenty dollars a month just to feed one like that."

"I wouldn't mind," Arch said. "I never had no dog."

" 'Sides," I said. "He got to belong to somebody."

"You think so?"

"Sure. A dog like that. *Some*body owns him."

"Well, if we just walk off," Arch said. "And he follows us. Now, that ain't stealin', is it?"

"I don't know," I said. "I guess not. Naw. That ain't stealin'."

By this time that first taco was gone. It was gone quick, in fact. In fact, it took two bites. And he was standin' there, Pest was. Just lookin' hungry. And grinnin'.

"If I buy three more tacos," Arch said, "and I just walk down the street, you think he'll follow me?"

"Looks likely."

"And that won't be stealin'?"

"I don't think so. Not a bit. You can't help what *he* does. Can you?"

"Naw, man. How can I help it?" Old Arch he went up to the window. "Give me three tacos," he said.

And that's the way we got Pest. I'll tell you in a minute the trouble we had keepin' him. And after that, I'll tell you how he saved old Arch's life. And mine, too. . . .

Keeping him turned out to be real trouble. Bit's father finally agreed the Pest could stay if Bit and Arch found a job to pay for the Pest's feed. But that wasn't easy. . . .

Next day it wasn't no different. I bet Arch and Pest and me walked twenty miles. I bet we went into a hundred stores and filling stations and places. I guess it was three-thirty, four o'clock we sank down to a curb over on Figueroa.

"Man, we had it," Arch said.

"Looks like."

"You think your old man, he really gonna make you—"

"My old man says somethin'," I said, "and he means it. He's fair but firm. You know what I mean?"

"I know," Arch said. "Yeah, I know."

Old Pest, he was watchin' us. He was watchin' us just like a man. Like he could understand. He come

over and kissed Arch. Then he gave me a lick on the
ear. Like he knew we was tryin' to keep him.

What do you think slid up in front of us, 'bout then?
This big black and white slab of metal. And this fancy
shield that says, "To serve and protect" on it. The red
light went to turnin' and flashin'. And this cop leaned
out the car window. "Hey," he says, "you boys got a
license for that dog?"

Arch and me, we jumped just about three feet.
"Man, yeah," Arch says, quick. "But we done left it at
home."

The cop laughed. "You better just run get it," he
says. "And make it quick."

Arch and me got a good look at him then. You know
how cops, they all look alike at first? Then you give 'em
a good look and they're some different, this one and
that one? We got a good look at this guy and it was
old Jimmy Hines.

"Hey, Jimmy," Arch says. "How's things?"

"What you boys up to?" Jimmy says. He grins.
"Kinda scared you, huh?"

"Yeah," Arch says, and, "Yeah," I says.

Old Jimmy's just like a little kid. I mean, he likes
flashin' that light and all that. He likes to sit behind
that siren. You know? So Arch and me, we go along.
"Yeah," we say.

"I hear you boys lookin' for a job."

Arch looked at him. "Who told you that?"

"Things get around," Jimmy says. He's white, but he's a good old boy. His partner, he's a black, I never did know his name. He's all right, too, Arch says. "We hear you got to support a dog."

"That's right," Arch says.

"He is a beauty," old Jimmy says. "I never saw a prettier dog." Old Jimmy, he's from Tennessee, but he's all right, too. "I like to have that dog," Jimmy says.

"Looks like you can, if you wants," Arch says. "Because we ain't never gonna find a job. Looks like. Today's the last day."

"Yeah," Jimmy says. He looked thoughtful. "You guys try over at Zimmerman's pet store?"

"Pet store?" I say. "Where's that?"

"Over on Imperial." . . .

"They really want some boys?" Arch says.

"Sure. Two boys to clean up and feed the animals. And water 'em, and like that. You know."

"Hey, great," I say.

"You better get on over there," Jim says.

"You know it, man," Arch tells him. And we're off.

The way we got friends with old Jimmy, it was like this. Arch and me was hittin' balls this Monday afternoon, out in the street in front of Arch's place. And old

Arch he really lays one out there. A long, low straight one. That hit a Ford headlight like it was aimed.

Now, most guys, they break somethin', they light out. And Arch and me *talked* about runnin', but we didn't. Arch said it wasn't right. So we stayed. We knowed the police would come. But we stayed. And sure enough, here come old Jim and his partner. Arch and Jim and this guy who owns the Ford, they talked it over. And Arch said he'd pay for the headlight, fifty cents a week. And he did. Ever since, old Jim, he sees us, we have a little talk. Like pass the time of day and that. You know.

Anyway, we got to Zimmerman's. And there was this lady behind the counter. She was real old, fifty or more.

"Hey, man, she looks mean," I whispered to Arch.

"Hush, man," Arch whispered back. "Who cares? We got to have the job. Ain't we?"

"We have got to have it."

We told Mrs. Zimmerman that Jimmy Hines sent us over. She looked us over through these big glasses of hers. Her eyes was black and hard as rocks.

"You boys don't steal," she said. "Do you steal?" She had this German accent. "You don't take things that don't belong to you?"

Arch and me, we shook our heads. "No ma'am," I said.

She gave us another long look. "And you work hard?"

"Yes ma'am," Arch, he said.

"You work two hours in the mornings," Mrs. Zimmerman said. "Six to eight. Cleaning cages. Feeding the animals. Giving water." She looked us over. "And two hours at night."

We nodded. I looked around. They was monkeys, six or eight of them. There was this thing I found out later. She called it a kinkajou. They was cats. And turtles. And mice. And rats. And parrots and other birds. And out back they was at least fifteen dogs, all kinds.

"You think you can do all this?" Mrs. Zimmerman said.

I looked around that place. And I thought uh-uh, I couldn't. But I looked at old Pest, and I thought un-huh, I could. "Yes ma'am," Arch said.

"Yes ma'am," I said.

"My August did it all," Mrs. Zimmerman said. "But now he is dead. He died two weeks ago. And by myself I can't do it."

"Yes ma'am," I said.

"So I give you five dollars a week."

Arch and me, we didn't say anything.

"Together," Mrs. Zimmerman said. "Five dollars together."

Arch and me, we looked at each other. It ain't much,

not for all that work. But what's a guy gonna do? "All right," Arch said. And I nod.

"Then shake on it," Mrs. Zimmerman said. And she shook hands with both of us. "Tomorrow morning," she said. "At six sharp."

I groaned inside. Me, I like to sleep late. Arch gets up real early. But I like to sleep as late as I can. Lord God. Six o'clock in the morning. I looked at Pest and I thought to myself, you better be worth it, old dog.

NEXT DOOR TO XANADU

by Doris Orgel

"What'll it be?" Mr. Gleisheimer asked.

He and I were the only ones in the store. Good, I thought, and hoped it would stay that way. I sat down at the counter.

He took a tall glass and a spoon with a long handle. He smiled. I smiled. It was sort of a joke between us, how he always asked me "What'll it be?"

I said, "The usual, please."

First he put chocolate syrup in. That looked so luscious I wished I could get a lick of it by itself. Next a squirt of milk. Then a stir. Then a whoosh of soda. As usual he let it bubble over the top. Then he wiped his hands on his apron, said *"Mmm"* as if it were finished, and waited for me to look disappointed. I grinned. I knew he wouldn't forget to top it off with a big dab of whipped cream—the real kind, not the kind from a can. There, now it was an egg cream. It is my favorite drink in the world. And Mr. Gleisheimer makes the best egg creams in Brooklyn.

Just as I was taking my first sip I heard the door open. "It may *not* be Bill Wexler," I told myself. (The thought of Bill gave me a bitter taste in my mouth; I had to take another big swallow of egg cream quick.) ". . . or Charlie Kriefer, or any of those."

But of course it *was* them, Bill and Charlie both. They asked for two nickel rolls of caps for their cap guns and for two fireballs.

I hunched way forward over the counter—as if that could keep them from seeing me! And I sipped, sipped, sipped, then took the straw out and gulped the rest of the egg cream down to fill myself up with sweetness before they spoiled it.

Then, just as I knew he would, Bill Wexler said, "Hey, Fatsy Patsy."

I didn't turn around.

"Why didn't you save a sip of that for little old devil

me?" "Little old devil" was supposed to remind me of Halloween—not that I was likely to forget *that*.

"Yeah, Fatsy Patsy," said Charlie Kriefer. He's Bill's personal parrot. "And you should have saved a sip for me!"

I still didn't turn around. I just sat and stared into my glass. I thought, If *only* I had a friend! If a friend sat here next to me, then Bill and Charlie could rank me, tease me, call me the dumbest names in the world. It wouldn't bother me a bit . . .

Mr. Gleisheimer handed them their caps and fire-balls.

"Let's go," said Bill.

But Charlie said, "Wait, I gotta catch up on my reading."

He leafed through a comic book, *Stratosphere Command*. Bill read over his shoulder. Then they looked through *Captain Colossal*. When they started on *Archie*, Mr. Gleisheimer cleared his throat. "Hey, boys," he said, "there's a library over by Fort Hamilton Parkway!"

"Okay, we get it. We're going," said Bill. "So long, Fatsy, see ya!"

I turned to see which way they were heading—across, not down, Prospect Park Southwest. I was safe. They wouldn't be hiding in wait for me somewhere on my way home. I saw them go into the entrance to Prospect Park, and I felt sorry for the birds and babies at whom they'd soon be shooting off their cap guns.

"Listen, Patricia, you ain't fat," said Mr. Gleisheimer as I was paying for my egg cream. "Don't mind them boys; they're just teasing. Here's something for you." He reached for the nearest thing on the candy counter and gave it to me for free to make me feel better.

I said, "Thanks, Mr. Gleisheimer," unwrapped it fast, and stuck it in my mouth. It did make me feel better. But then I looked down at the wrapper in my hand. It said "Chunky." That's what the candy was—and so was I!

I left feeling as fat as Galoomphy. She's the female hippopotamus in Prospect Park Zoo. If only, *only* I was thin! I felt really miserable walking home until I saw the truck. It was a huge one. It stood in exactly the right place—right in front of 600 Greenwood Avenue. That's the apartment house I live in. And another good sign was that it was orange and black, Halloween colors! So I couldn't help thinking that maybe my spell from Halloween *was* starting to work.

I was ten years old then (I'm almost eleven now, or

I will be in September). I was four feet four inches, not very tall for my age. My hair is brown, medium long. My mother calls it honey-brown, and she says she envies the way it turns under or out depending on which way I comb it. My eyes are brown too. The color of hazelnuts, my mother says. And when she used to try really hard to build up my self-confidence about the way I looked, she'd tell me I had nice, long eyelashes and that my face was finely shaped. So what if my *face* was, who cared? The rest of me wasn't; that's what mattered. I had weighed eighty-nine and a half pounds on Dr. Baumgarten's scale at my checkup last September. I can still hear how he clicked his tongue, *Tsk, tsk!* And he said, "You'll have to watch what you eat, Patricia, and lose some of this." Then he pinched a handful of the "this" around my middle. I felt like pinching him back; he isn't a skinny person himself. But he was right. I was pretty fat, or kids wouldn't have called me those dumb, awful names.

Oh, they didn't always do it to my face. Karen Latham, Betsy Weiss—girls like that—and some of the boys too tried not to. And if one of them did by accident, somebody said, "Shush, she can hear you!" I minded that almost more than the names. But I knew how not to show it. And I wasn't the outcast of Greenwood Avenue either. I got along pretty well with a lot of kids—even if I wasn't exactly friends with them.

Besides, I had lots of people I liked in books, for instance, Connie Ives in *The Alley*. And the little mermaid in Andersen—well, she wasn't exactly "people," but I didn't care. And Alice, of course, and Anna Lavinia from *Beyond the Paw-paw Trees*. Hundreds. And I thought any one of them was better company than all the kids in this building, neighborhood, and P.S. 397 put together.

Besides, my parents were pretty great (they still are, but I'm thinking about *then*).

Besides, I had Susan—at last! Of course she was only four months old, and all she could do was eat, sleep, suck her thumb or bottle, make BM's in her diapers, cry, and smile. But I knew she would do more and be better company as time went on.

There were lots of "besideses" like that in my life. It wasn't *all* loneliness and eating my heart out, as Mom put it. (I heard her say that one night when she and Daddy were talking about how I didn't have any friends.)

But the trouble with "besideses" is they're beside the point. And the point, I used to think, was right in my name—not just what Pat rhymes with, but also what's left when you leave the *M* off Malone.

I used to think about that a lot. And every time I did, I'd end up in the kitchen, standing on a chair because Mom finally put the jar on the highest shelf in the cabinet, and I'd grab a Fig Newton, chocolate-covered graham crackers, and a Mallomar or two.

Mallomars remind me of Halloween. Even with the treat part, that's one holiday I've never really looked forward to. But Mom made me a black cardboard witch's hat. It came out really good. And she lent me a black dress of hers. And she went out and bought eye shadow to make my whole face green. So I couldn't *not* go trick-or-treating.

Besides, I couldn't let the kids in the building—who always trick-or-treat in twos, threes, and fours—think I minded going by myself.

So I put all that stuff on and started next door at 2C, where the Misses Osteroff lived. Miss Edith Osteroff worked in a cleaning store on Prospect Avenue. Miss Ida Osteroff worked in an office in downtown Brooklyn. Miss Ida opened the door for me. She gave me three Mallomars and a handful of candy corn.

I thanked her. Then I went across the hall to apartment 2A, where the Wexlers, our other next-door neighbors, live. They have three children: my old tormentor, Bill (he's eleven and a half now), and

Marshall (he's three), and Sherman (he's a year and a half).

I was sure Bill was out trick-or-treating—mostly tricking—with Charlie Kriefer and his other friends. I never thought he might be home.

I rang the bell. The door flew open. But I didn't see anybody. It was all dark in the Wexlers' foyer. Suddenly there was an awful shout of "TRICK *and* TREAT!" right in my ear, and this devil came jumping at me. He had horns on his head, a pitchfork, and a tail. He nearly knocked me down. My hat fell off. I got so scared, and then I got so ashamed for being scared I couldn't even shout anything back. I bent to pick up my hat. That's when he pinned me down with the pitchfork. With his other hand he grabbed the candy corn I was holding and stuffed it into his mouth. He took the Mallomars too. "*You* shouldn't eat all those sweets," he said, "Fatsy Pat," or maybe "Patsy Fat"—I wasn't sure which, I ran home so fast.

Mom was sitting in our foyer, facing the other way, giving Susan her bottle. She didn't see what a mess I was.

I wiped my eyes with my sleeve. It got all green from the makeup. I said, "I hate Halloween! And I hate Bill Wexler. He can go to hell!"

"Now wait a minute." Mom turned around to me.

"Well, he can. He's a devil," I said. And I told what he had done.

Mom put Susan in her playpen. She got the eye shadow and covered up the streaks on my face. She taped my hat back together where it was ripped. Then she brought me a broom. "You go right back out there," she said. "And if any more devils bother you, use the broom on them."

So I went out to trick-or-treat some more. But first I stood perfectly still outside apartment 2A, and I swore —by the broom, black cats and kettles, eyes of newts— that someday I'd get revenge on Bill.

But then I asked myself, "How? How would I ever be able to, alone, with him stronger than me, and me scared of him?" I couldn't answer. I squeezed my eyes shut, crossed my fingers, held my breath, and wished— the same old wish—that I had a friend, a girl my age who wouldn't care whether I was fat and who'd never call me anything but my right name. I wished she'd move right into this building, into an apartment right on this floor, right into here, next door to me. And why not help the wish along a little, trace a hex sign, cast a spell? After all, it wasn't every day I had a green face, a witch's costume, and a broom in my hand. So I traced a hex sign in the air, made up a spell, and cast it:

WEXLERS, WEXLERS, MOVE AWAY
FROM APARTMENT TWO—OO—A!

Four days after Halloween, Saturday morning on my
way home from Gleisheimer's, I saw that moving
truck!

"It can't be for the Wexlers," I told myself. "Bill
wouldn't be fooling around in the park if they were
moving today. It's probably some people on the fifth
or sixth floor."

But wait a minute—I knew that little table on the
sidewalk with the carved lion paws for feet. I'd seen
that table before, somewhere. . . . A moving man lifted
it into the truck. Then I remembered, in the Misses
Osteroff's foyer when I trick-or-treated there. So Miss
Edith and Miss Ida were the people who were moving
out!

They stopped by later to say good-bye to us. "We're
retiring," Miss Edith said.

"Yes," said Miss Ida, "we're going to live with our
brother on his chicken farm in Middletown."

Apartment 2C, next door, was free!

All next Monday, Tuesday, and Wednesday, painters painted the walls in there. On Thursday, floor

scrapers came and scraped and varnished the floors. They worked with the front door open. I stood and watched them for a while when I came home from school. And twice while I was practicing the piano, I got up, went out into the hall, and took some whiffs of the smell of fresh paint and varnish.

I loved that smell. It suited the way I was feeling. This may sound peculiar, but it was a lot like the lefthand chords you play to accompany a tune. And the tune was the hope-wait-wish feeling inside myself.

I tried to make it stop. I made myself think back to last year when I was nine, to what can happen if you hope-wait-wish too hard. Apartment 2G down the other end of the hall had been empty. I'd been waiting and waiting for new people to move in. Then they did move in, the Weisses, with Betsy, and she looked about nine like me!

So I rushed over there and asked her to play with me. She didn't know anybody yet; she was glad to. She showed me how great she was at skipping rope—one hundred and twelve times without missing! Then we played jacks. Betsy's crazy about jacks. So for about two weeks all I did was skip rope—not too well, but I hoped to improve—and play jacks, jacks, jacks, as if there weren't any other games in the world.

Then the Lathams, who live in 2F, came home from their vacation. And Karen Latham's a much better rope-skipper than me, and she doesn't just pretend she likes to play jacks. That was the end of Betsy's being friends with me. Once in a while she or Karen still asked me to play with them, especially if Mrs. Weiss or Mrs. Latham told them to. But it wasn't much fun. It never is for a third person barging in.

But even while I was thinking about all that, I kept hearing the hope-wait-wish tune. I couldn't make it stop, even after the painters and scrapers were done next door and the smell of paint and varnish had faded.

On Friday instead of practicing, I tried to get the tune out of myself and onto the piano. I fooled around in different keys, with different notes. I tried it slow, fast, in between. The way I heard it inside me it sounded very serious, almost like a hymn, but also full of ripples like a lake you want to swim in. No matter what I did, I couldn't make it come out like that.

I gave up on the tune, and instead I put words to the scales I was supposed to practice. That was much easier. "A girl my age will move next door," I sang to myself in C Major, G Major, B-flat Major, and F Major, ascending and descending.

I sang it so many times Mom finally called, "That's

enough scales! Play your Bartok and your Haydn sona-
tina now!"

The next morning I went to Gleisheimer's, as I always did on Saturdays. Coming back, I counted how
many steps it would take from the candy store to the
corner. If the number had a seven in it or if it was a
multiple of seven, that meant a girl my age was going
to move in next door. Forty-eight, forty-nine, fifty,
fifty-one—I was getting near—fifty-two, -three, -four,
-five—I was really there already, but I took another step
just to make it come out fifty-six, eight times seven.
But that last step was really cheating.

I started another test, a harder one—walking through
the empty lot with my eyes closed without falling over
anything or bumping into anything all the way. I held
my arms out in front of me and started to walk. I tried
to picture in my mind all the bits and wrecks of things
I knew I had to avoid—the mattress springs, the broken
baby carriage, the bicycle tires, cartons, cans, an old
stove, part of a bathtub, all the rocks and rubble this
"empty" lot was full of.

"Hey, Patsy!" someone called from the other side of
Greenwood Avenue. I recognized the voice. It was
Betsy's. "Are you walking in your sleep or some-
thing?"

Mind your own business, I thought, and called, "Yes, I'm sleepwalking, and if you wake me it's seven years' bad luck!" Just then my left hand touched something cold—the edge of the old bathtub. That meant not much farther to go.

"In five more steps I'll open my eyes—and there'll be a moving truck," I promised myself. "Just like last week. That'll be a sure sign a girl my age is moving into 2C."

Five steps and I opened my eyes. But in front of 600 Greenwood stood only old Mr. Montecapecchi, his black-and-white horse, and his vegetable cart. I like Mr. Montecapecchi, and I usually pet the horse—but not now, not when they were taking up the moving truck's whole parking space! Probably the truck driver was driving around and around the block this very minute with the new next-door neighbors' furniture in the truck, waiting till he could park in front of the building.

"No, that's dumb!" I told myself. "Probably no-body's moving in this morning. Anyway, tests like that can't really prove anything."

But that afternoon I made up another test, with Susan in it. She was in her playpen on her stomach, looking at the design of teddy bears parading up and down the playpen mat.

I got down on my knees, stuck my face in through the bars, and said very seriously, "A ten-year-old girl will move in next door, and she and I will be friends. True or false?"

If Susan smiled, that would mean true. If she frowned or started to cry, false. But she just looked at me with her big blue eyes and didn't smile *or* frown.

"*Chirp, chirp, tweet!*" I made bird noises and flapped my hands like wings, and that got her laughing all right. But I really did it more for the fun of it than to influence the test.

So then I ran the test five more times without interfering. The results were two smiles, two frowns, and once Susan started to cry—but that was just before her dinnertime, which is her usual hour to crab.

Sunday night I was standing in Mom and Daddy's bedroom beside Susan's crib, and I tried the test again. Susan was bored with the whole thing. She tried to grab one of the butterflies from her butterfly mobile, and she wouldn't even look at me. But Mom had tiptoed in. She hugged me. She must have overheard the whole test. "Oh, Patricia, I hope the answer's Yes," she whispered. "Just don't be too disappointed if . . . if . . ."—she looked worried for me—then she smiled and said, "if a Mr. and Mrs. Pimpampanilla move in next door with quintuplets, all boys, all awful teases!"

Monday I got home from school. I plunked my books down on a chair in the foyer. I was on my way to the kitchen for cookies and soda, if there was any, when the bell rang. I opened the door. And there she stood!

She had gray eyes. I could see their color even out in the dim hall. She had brown braids; one of them was coming undone. She was a little taller and a lot thinner than me, and beautiful in a pair of faded jeans and an old plaid shirt. She said, "You're Patricia Malone. I was here this morning. Your mother said you were ten. Me too."

I just stared. I thought, It's too good. It can't be. It was though.

"We moved in there this morning"—she meant 2C —"and I'm in the middle of unpacking. Oh, I haven't told you my name. I'm Dorothy Rap—"

Something flew into my head about her name, and before I knew it I'd said it aloud, "Next-Dorothy!"

"What did you say?"

I started to feel embarrassed. "Well, you see, I've sort of been wishing a girl my age would move in next door, and you did, so I called you Next-Dorothy." I felt like a fool, and shaky like somebody out on a high branch of a tall tree. What if she thought this was silly? What if this Next-Dorothy was already friends with some other kids in the building? What if she had heard my nicknames? What if she didn't want to be friends?

"Do you think that's a dumb name?" I asked.

"No, I like it. I just can't stand it when people call me Dot, or Dotty, or Dodo. I think those are really dumb, don't you?"

"Oh, I do! I feel the same about people calling me Patsy for short, or Pat, or . . ." I didn't mention the worst ones. "Come on in!"

"I was already in your house, I mean your apartment. I can't get used to saying 'apartment.' I've always lived in houses before. Your mother gave me some soda, and I met your baby sister while you were at school. So now you come see our apartment, okay?"

"Sure! Mom, I'm going next door with Dorothy!" I shouted, and didn't even wait for her to call back "All right" or anything.

Their foyer was full of suitcases, crates, and laundry bags. A tall man sat on the floor in the middle of a pile of books.

"Daddy, this is Patricia Malone. She lives in 2B," Dorothy said. "Patricia, this is my father."

Professor Rappaport stood up to greet me—as if I were a lady! He shook my hand and said, "I'm happy to meet you," and sounded like he really meant it.

"Now Ag!" Dorothy grabbed my other hand and pulled me into the kitchen. "Ag, look. This is Patricia Malone from next door!"

A lady with gray hair climbed down a stepladder. "Apartment-house-living advantage number one," she said. "Didn't I tell you, Dorothy?"

"Oh, Ag!" Dorothy looked embarrassed.

Ag looked me over. "Nice to know you, Pat."

"Not Pat. Her name's Patricia," said Dorothy.

"Okay, okay. Have a doughnut, Patricia." Ag put a bakery bag on the table. "You two sit down and get acquainted. I'll go see if I can help the professor get out from under those bundles and books."

Dorothy and I sat down, and right away I reached for the bag. But then I really surprised myself. I pulled my arm back. I was *not* going to have a doughnut. I wasn't even going to look and see if by any chance there were jelly doughnuts in the bag.

"Her name's really Agnes," Dorothy was saying. "That means lamb—some lamb! She's more like a bear, the way she clumps down a ladder. And sometimes she's like a mule, so stubborn you just can't budge her. Still and all, she's a good old thing."

"Is she your aunt or who?" I asked.

"No. She keeps house for us, and cooks, and takes care of me—not that I don't take care of *myself* pretty well."

I tried to ask something else. "What about your—"

She kept on talking. "My father's a professor at Brooklyn College. That's why we moved here from

Great Neck. He got too tired driving back and forth every day on the Long Island Expressway. Before we lived in Great Neck, we lived in Poughkeepsie, and before that, when I was about two years old, we lived in Edinburgh, Scotland."

"Yes, but what about your—"

"My mother's dead," said Dorothy.

My face got hot. I shouldn't have asked a thing like that. I wanted to tell her how sorry I was. I started to stutter. "Oh . . . er . . ."

"Don't. You don't have to," said Dorothy. "People always think they should say something, but it's really okay. She died when I was a baby. I don't even remember her."

I tried to think how that must feel. I didn't know what to say.

"Hey, Patricia, don't you want a doughnut?"

I'd forgotten about them. But now, oh, sure, I wanted one! I said, "Yes, but I'm not having one."

"How come?"

"Because I'm too fat," I said, not looking at her.

"You are not!"

That's what she said! I felt like hugging her. "Well, you should hear what kids call me." I started to tell— then I couldn't. I pushed the bag over to her. "You haven't had a doughnut either."

"No, I've been too busy talking." She took one. It was a jelly doughnut!

My mouth started to water. My fingers itched. Then I thought, That bag of doughnuts is like those tests I made up. A girl my age *had* moved next door. Now if I left that bag of doughnuts alone, that would mean she'd really be and stay my friend.

I swallowed hard. I didn't take a doughnut.

Dorothy ate hers and kept on talking. She told me what their house was like in Great Neck, about the brand-new school there, and about her teacher, Mrs. Royce. Mrs. Royce was possibly the third-ugliest person in the entire world, Dorothy said. She told about some kids in her class. Then she started to tell me about the Neilsons—they'd been the Rappaports' neighbors. But she stopped and said, "I do talk a lot, don't I?"

Yes, she did, and the more, the better, I thought. I wanted to hear everything about her.

"Go on," I said. "Tell about the Neilsons."

She suddenly looked so sad that I asked, "Do you miss them a lot?"

"Oh, no, they were about Ag's age. *She* misses them. I miss Mauberley."

"Who's Mauberley?"

"Our cat. I mean he *was* our cat."

I said, "I know just how you feel."

Then we went into her room because she wanted to show me a photograph of Mauberley. She dumped things out of a suitcase till she found it.

"Oh, he's beautiful!" I said.

"And we had to give him to the Neilsons!"

"Why did you have to?"

"Because Ag wouldn't let him come with us. She just wouldn't. She said he'd never get used to being cooped up in an apartment. That's apartment-house-living *dis*advantage number one!" She banged the suitcase shut and sat on it. She wrinkled up her fore-head, thinking of Mauberley, I guess. "Hey, Patricia, have *you* got a cat?" she asked.

I wished I could have said Yes. I shook my head. "My mother says a baby's enough, and we don't need a cat around too. By the way, what's apartment-house-living *ad*vantage number one?"

"Having kids my age right in the same building. In Great Neck most of the kids I liked lived too far away to walk to. Listen, what's your favorite num-ber?"

"Seven. Yours?"

"Seven!"

We both laughed. I wasn't really surprised though. Somehow I knew she'd say seven.

"By the way," said Dorothy, "is Greenwood Avenue anywhere near Myrtle?"

At first I thought she meant because of the Myrtle Avenue El. I said, "No, it's pretty far. But the regular subway goes above the streets for a few blocks right near here. You'll go on it when you go to Manhat—" I stopped suddenly because I thought she might have asked for another reason. It just might be . . . so I said, "You mean because of the Myrtle Avenue that's near The Alley?"

"Yes! I loved reading *The Alley*! You too? I even wanted my father to get a job teaching at Grandby College—"

"That's a made-up name," I told her. "It's really called Pratt Institute, but everything else is the same as in the book—the little houses where the teachers and their families live and the campus with the flagpole and the old cannon. You'll see it. I'll get my mother to take us there . . ."

Now we both were talking a lot, and fast because there was such a lot to say. Every minute or so we found out about another thing we had in common. I think we got to know each other better in that one afternoon than some people do in whole weeks and months. Still, the time went so fast we were surprised when Ag called, "Dorothy, wash up for dinner."

Ag came in. "Holy Jehoshaphat!" she yelled. "Will you look at this room! In all this time you haven't picked up a thing! Ah, well, whatever *I* don't do in this family . . ."

She wasn't *too* mad though, or she wouldn't have invited me to stay for dinner. "Go ask your mother, Patricia," she said. "We've got plenty, and you'd be very welcome."

"Go ahead, and come right back!" said Dorothy.

I said, "I'd love to!" But then I thought how late it was, and I hadn't practiced yet. Also, I had three pages of fractions to do for arithmetic homework. "No, I guess I can't," I said, but I thanked Ag for inviting me. "I'll see you tomorrow, Dorothy. Be ready by twenty to nine. No, better make it eight-thirty; I'll call for you."

"Okay. Good night, Patricia."

"Good night," I said. And I knew it would be.

It was! I curled up under my old quilt with a book in front of me as usual. But I couldn't keep my mind on it, even though I'd just come to an interesting part where this girl and her brother run away from home to go live in the Metropolitan Museum of Art. I read the same sentence six times. I finally put the book down and just lay there thinking . . .

Other nights at nine-thirty, which is when I'm sup-

posed to stop reading and go to sleep, I sometimes had
such an empty feeling in my stomach I'd get up for a
snack even though I'd have to brush my teeth again
and be cold again when I got back into bed. But that
night I just thought about Dorothy's living next door
now and about things we'd be doing together, and I
felt so good I didn't even want a snack.

After a while I began to want a Mallomar or something. But then I thought of the jelly doughnut I
hadn't had at Dorothy's. Too bad I couldn't put it in a
frame with a sign, "The First Jelly Doughnut I Ever
Said No To," and hang it up over my bed!

"From now on I'll say No to Mallomars, Fig New-
tons, candy, and lots of things, not just jelly doughnuts." I made myself that solemn promise. Then I
turned over on my stomach and went to sleep.

STUART LITTLE

by E. B. White

When Mrs. Frederick C. Little's second son arrived,
everybody noticed that he was not much bigger than a
mouse. The truth of the matter was, the baby looked
very much like a mouse in every way. He was only
about two inches high; and he had a mouse's sharp
nose, a mouse's tail, a mouse's whiskers, and the pleas-
ant, shy manner of a mouse. Before he was many days
old he was not only looking like a mouse but acting

like one, too—wearing a gray hat and carrying a small cane. Mr. and Mrs. Little named him Stuart . . .

One morning when the wind was from the west, Stuart put on his sailor suit and his sailor hat, took his spyglass down from the shelf, and set out for a walk, full of the joy of life and the fear of dogs. With a rolling gait he sauntered along toward Fifth Avenue, keeping a sharp lookout.

Whenever he spied a dog through his glass, Stuart would hurry to the nearest doorman, climb his trouser-leg, and hide in the tails of his uniform. And once, when no doorman was handy, he had to crawl into a yesterday's paper and roll himself up in the second section till danger was past.

At the corner of Fifth Avenue there were several people waiting for the uptown bus, and Stuart joined them. Nobody noticed him, because he wasn't tall enough to be noticed.

"I'm not tall enough to be noticed," thought Stuart, "yet I'm tall enough to want to go to Seventy-second Street."

When the bus came into view, all the men waved their canes and brief cases at the driver, and Stuart waved his spyglass. Then, knowing that the step of the bus would be too high for him, Stuart seized hold of the cuff of a gentleman's pants and was swung aboard without any trouble or inconvenience whatever.

Stuart never paid any fare on buses, because he wasn't big enough to carry an ordinary dime. The only time he had every attempted to carry a dime, he had rolled the coin along like a hoop while he raced along beside it; but it had got away from him on a hill and had been snatched up by an old woman with no teeth. After that experience Stuart contented himself with the tiny coins which his father made for him out of tin foil. They were handsome little things, although rather hard to see without putting on your spectacles.

When the conductor came around to collect the fares, Stuart fished in his purse and pulled out a coin no bigger than the eye of a grasshopper.

"What's that you're offering me?" asked the conductor.

"It's one of my dimes," said Stuart.

"Is it, now?" said the conductor. "Well, I'd have a fine time explaining that to the bus company. Why, you're no bigger than a dime yourself."

"Yes I am," replied Stuart angrily. "I'm more than twice as big as a dime. A dime only comes up to here on me." And Stuart pointed to his hip. "Furthermore," he added, "I didn't come on this bus to be insulted."

"I beg pardon," said the conductor. "You'll have to

forgive me, for I had no idea that in all the world there was such a small sailor."

"Live and learn," muttered Stuart, tartly, putting his change purse back in his pocket.

When the bus stopped at Seventy-second Street, Stuart jumped out and hurried across to the sailboat pond in Central Park. Over the pond the west wind blew, and into the teeth of the west wind sailed the sloops and schooners, their rails well down, their wet decks gleaming. The owners, boys and grown men, raced around the cement shores hoping to arrive at the other side in time to keep the boats from bumping. Some of the toy boats were not as small as you might think, for when you got close to them you found that their mainmast was taller than a man's head, and they were beautifully made, with everything shipshape and ready for sea. To Stuart they seemed enormous, and he hoped he would be able to get aboard one of them and sail away to the far corners of the pond. (He was an adventurous little fellow and loved the feel of the breeze in his face and the cry of the gulls overhead and the heave of the great swell under him.)

As he sat cross-legged on the wall that surrounds the pond, gazing out at the ships through his spyglass, Stuart noticed one boat that seemed to him finer and prouder than any other. Her name was Wasp. She was a big, black schooner flying the American flag. She had a clipper bow, and on her foredeck was mounted a three-inch cannon. She's the ship for me, thought Stuart. And the next time she sailed in, he ran over to where she was being turned around.

"Excuse me, sir," said Stuart to the man who was turning her, "but are you the owner of the schooner Wasp?"

"I am," replied the man, surprised to be addressed by a mouse in a sailor suit.

"I'm looking for a berth in a good ship," continued Stuart, "and I thought perhaps you might sign me on. I'm strong and I'm quick."

"Are you sober?" asked the owner of the Wasp.

"I do my work," said Stuart, crisply.

The man looked sharply at him. He couldn't help admiring the trim appearance and bold manner of this diminutive seafaring character.

"Well," he said at length, pointing the prow of the Wasp out toward the center of the pond, "I'll tell you what I'll do with you. You see that big racing sloop out there?"

"I do," said Stuart.

"That's the Lillian B. Womrath," said the man, "and I hate her with all my heart."

"Then so do I," cried Stuart, loyally.

"I hate her because she is always bumping into my

boat," continued the man, "and because her owner is a lazy boy who doesn't understand sailing and who hardly knows a squall from a squid."

"Or a jib from a jibe," cried Stuart.

"Or a luff from a leech," bellowed the man.

"Or a deck from a dock," screamed Stuart.

"Or a mast from a mist," yelled the man. "But hold on, now, no more of this! I'll tell you what we'll do. The Lillian B. Womrath has always been able to beat the Wasp sailing, but I believe that if my schooner were properly handled it would be a different story. Nobody knows how I suffer, standing here on shore, helpless, watching the Wasp blunder along, when all she needs is a steady hand on her helm. So, my young friend, I'll let you sail the Wasp across the pond and back, and if you can beat that detestable sloop I'll give you a regular job."

"Aye, aye, sir!" said Stuart, swinging himself aboard the schooner and taking his place at the wheel. "Ready about!"

"One moment," said the man. "Do you mind telling me *how* you propose to beat the other boat?"

"I intend to crack on more sail," said Stuart.

"Not in *my* boat, thank you," replied the man quickly. "I don't want you capsizing in a squall."

"Well, then," said Stuart, "I'll catch the sloop

broad on, and rake her with fire from my forward gun."

"Foul means!" said the man. "I want this to be a boat race, not a naval engagement."

"Well, then," said Stuart cheerfully, "I'll sail the Wasp straight and true, and let the Lillian B. Womrath go yawing all over the pond."

"Bravo!" cried the man, "and good luck go with you!" And so saying, he let go of the Wasp's prow. A puff of air bellied out the schooner's headsails and she paid off and filled away on the port tack, heeling gracefully over to the breeze while Stuart twirled her wheel and braced himself against a deck cleat.

"By the by," yelled the man, "you haven't told me your name."

"Name is Stuart Little," called Stuart at the top of his lungs. "I'm the second son of Frederick C. Little, of this city."

"*Bon voyage*, Stuart," hollered his friend, "take care of yourself and bring the Wasp home safe."

"That I will," shouted Stuart. And he was so proud and happy, he let go of the wheel for a second and did a little dance on the sloping deck, never noticing how narrowly he escaped hitting a tramp steamer that was drifting in his path, with her engines disabled and her decks awash.

When the people in Central Park learned that one of the toy sailboats was being steered by a mouse in a sailor suit, they all came running. Soon the shores of the pond were so crowded that a policeman was sent from headquarters to announce that everybody would have to stop pushing, but nobody did. People in New York like to push each other. The most excited person of all was the boy who owned the Lillian B. Womrath. He was a fat, sulky boy of twelve, named LeRoy. He wore a blue serge suit and a white necktie stained with orange juice.

"Come back here!" he called to Stuart. "Come back here and get on *my* boat. I want you to steer *my* boat. I will pay you five dollars a week and you can have every Thursday afternoon off and a radio in your room."

"I thank you for your kind offer," replied Stuart, "but I am happy aboard the Wasp—happier than I have ever been before in all my life." And with that he spun the wheel over smartly and headed his schooner down toward the starting line, where LeRoy was turning his boat around by poking it with a long stick, ready for the start of the race.

"I'll be the referee," said a man in a bright green suit. "Is the Wasp ready?"

"Ready, sir!" shouted Stuart, touching his hat.

"Is the Lillian B. Womrath ready?" asked the referee.

"Sure, I'm ready," said LeRoy.

"To the north end of the pond and back again!" shouted the referee. "On your mark, get set, GO!"

"Go!" cried the people along the shore.

"Go!" cried the owner of the Wasp.

"Go!" yelled the policeman.

And away went the two boats for the north end of the pond, while the seagulls wheeled and cried overhead and the taxicabs tooted and honked from Seventy-second Street and the west wind (which had come halfway across America to get to Central Park) sang and whistled in the rigging and blew spray across the decks, stinging Stuart's cheeks with tiny fragments of flying peanut shell tossed up from the foamy deep. "This is the life for me!" Stuart murmured to himself. "What a ship! What a day! What a race!"

Before the two boats had gone many feet, however, an accident happened on shore. The people were pushing each other harder and harder in their eagerness to see the sport, and although they really didn't mean to, they pushed the policeman so hard they pushed him right off the concrete wall and into the pond. He hit the water in a sitting position, and got wet clear up to the third button of his jacket. He was soaked.

This particular policeman was not only a big, heavy man, but he had just eaten a big, heavy meal, and the wave he made went curling outward, cresting and billowing, upsetting all manner of small craft and causing every owner of a boat on the pond to scream with delight and consternation.

When Stuart saw the great wave approaching he jumped for the rigging, but he was too late. Towering above the Wasp like a mountain, the wave came crashing and piling along the deck, caught Stuart up and swept him over the side and into the water, where everybody supposed he would drown. Stuart had no intention of drowning. He kicked hard with his feet, and thrashed hard with his tail, and in a minute or two he climbed back aboard the schooner, cold and wet but quite unharmed. As he took his place at the helm, he could hear people cheering for him and calling, "Atta mouse, Stuart! Atta mouse!" He looked over and saw that the wave had capsized the Lillian B. Womrath but that she had righted herself and was sailing on her course, close by. And she stayed close alongside till both boats reached the north end of the pond. Here Stuart put the Wasp about and LeRoy turned the Lillian around with his stick, and away the two boats went for the finish line.

"This race isn't over yet," thought Stuart.

The first warning he had that there was trouble

ahead came when he glanced into the Wasp's cabin and observed that the barometer had fallen sharply. That can mean only one thing at sea—dirty weather. Suddenly a dark cloud swept across the sun, blotting it out and leaving the earth in shadow. Stuart shivered in his wet clothes. He turned up his sailor blouse closer around his neck, and when he spied the Wasp's owner among the crowd on shore he waved his hat and called out:

"Dirty weather ahead, sir! Wind backing into the south-west, seas confused, glass falling."

"Never mind the weather!" cried the owner. "Watch out for flotsam dead ahead!"

Stuart peered ahead into the gathering storm, but saw nothing except gray waves with white crests. The world seemed cold and ominous. Stuart glanced behind him. There came the sloop, boiling along fast, rolling up a bow wave and gaining steadily.

"Look out, Stuart! Look out where you're going!"

Stuart strained his eyes, and suddenly, dead ahead, right in the path of the Wasp, he saw an enormous paper bag looming up on the surface of the pond. The bag was empty and riding high, its open end gaping wide like the mouth of a cave. Stuart spun the wheel over but it was too late: the Wasp drove her bowsprit straight into the bag and with a fearful *whooosh* the schooner slowed down and came up into the wind with all sails flapping. Just at this moment Stuart heard a splintering crash, saw the bow of the Lillian plow through his rigging, and felt the whole ship tremble from stem to stern with the force of the collision.

"A collision!" shouted the crowd on shore.

In a jiffy the two boats were in a terrible tangle. Little boys on shore screamed and danced up and down. Meanwhile the paper bag sprang a leak and began to fill.

The Wasp couldn't move because of the bag. The Lillian B. Womrath couldn't move because her nose was stuck in the Wasp's rigging.

Waving his arms, Stuart ran forward and fired off his gun. Then he heard, above the other voices on shore, the voice of the owner of the Wasp yelling directions and telling him what to do.

"Stuart! Stuart! Down jib! Down staysail!"

Stuart jumped for the halyards, and the jib and the forestaysail came rippling down.

"Cut away all paper bags!" roared the owner.

Stuart whipped out his pocketknife and slashed away bravely at the soggy bag until he had the deck cleared.

"Now back your foresail and give her a full!" screamed the owner of the Wasp.

Stuart grabbed the foresail boom and pulled with all his might. Slowly the schooner paid off and began to gather headway. And as she heeled over to the breeze she rolled her rail out from under the Lillian's nose, shook herself free, and stood away to the southard. A loud cheer went up from the bank. Stuart sprang to the wheel and answered it. Then he looked back, and to his great joy he perceived that the Lillian had gone off in a wild direction and was yawing all over the pond.

Straight and true sailed the Wasp, with Stuart at the helm. After she had crossed the finish line, Stuart brought her alongside the wall, and was taken ashore and highly praised for his fine seamanship and daring. The owner was delighted and said it was the happiest day of his life. He introduced himself to Stuart, said that in private life he was Dr. Paul Carey, a surgeon-dentist. He said model boats were his hobby and that he would be delighted to have Stuart take command of his vessel at any time. Everybody shook hands with Stuart—everybody, that is, except the policeman, who was too wet and mad to shake hands with a mouse.

When Stuart got home that night, his brother George asked him where he had been all day.

"Oh, knocking around town," replied Stuart.

THE PROMISED YEAR

by Yoshiko Uchida

Living with Aunt Emi and Uncle Henry in San Francisco was not at all like being at home in Japan. Keiko was homesick. To make matters worse, she was responsible for a cat, and Uncle Henry did not like cats.

Keiko hurried from her room the next morning and discovered that Uncle Henry had already eaten and gone to take a shipment of flowers to the airport.

"I've been waiting for you," Aunt Emi said cheerfully, and she took a pan of piping-hot golden-brown biscuits from the oven.

"Now, have some orange juice," she urged, "and I'll make you some bacon and eggs. I do want you to start off your second day in America with a good breakfast."

She bustled back and forth between the big white refrigerator and the table, bringing out butter and honey and strawberry jam and cream, spreading everything out in front of Keiko at the table. Keiko knew she could love Aunt Emi without any trouble at all, but Uncle Henry was another matter entirely.

Keiko hurried to the laundry for just a quick look to see if Tama was all right, but when she looked in, the carton was empty. "Where's Tama?" she asked, and quickly she checked the other rooms. "I don't see Tama anywhere," she said to her aunt.

Aunt Emi slipped a plate of sizzling bacon and a sunny-side-up egg in front of her and told her to hurry and eat before everything got cold. When she saw that Keiko had begun to eat, she explained, "Uncle Henry thought Tama would be happier outside last night, so he let her out. I'm sure she'll be home as soon as she gets hungry."

Keiko agreed that she thought she would, and for a while, until she had eaten three biscuits dripping with butter and honey, she didn't feel worried at all about Tama. She licked the sticky sweetness from around her mouth, and when Aunt Emi wasn't looking, she even licked the honey that had stuck to her knife. But before long, Keiko began to wonder just how long cats stayed away before they came home for breakfast.

"Aunt Emi," she said, "do you think Tama might like some dried fish?"

Aunt Emi nodded. "I think she might at that," she answered. "I'll get you some I bought from Mr. Ito's grocery truck just last week." And then she saw how worried Keiko was and suggested she take the fish out on the back porch. "You just sit on the steps with those dried mackerel for a while," she said, laughing, "and you'll probably have every cat in the neighborhood, as well as Tama, coming to beg for some."

As Keiko started outside, Aunt Emi called after her, "Don't go off too far now. As soon as your uncle gets back from the airport, we're going to San Francisco."

"I won't," Keiko answered, but it was the kind of proper answer she could give without having listened at all to what came before it. She was very good at that because Grandmother was always telling her to watch out for Kenbo or to come home before it got dark or to wash her hands before she ate, and Keiko always managed to give the right answer even though she had only half heard what Grandmother said.

Clutching her dried fish in one hand now, Keiko started down the back steps and out toward the greenhouses. Surely Tama must be somewhere nearby. Keiko went to the shed where Uncle Henry kept his rotor tiller and his tractor and his flower pots and sacks of fertilizer.

"Tama," she called into the shadowy stillness, but nothing moved except a butterfly that struggled up toward the sky.

Next Keiko went up and down between the greenhouses. She climbed over old coils of hose and wire, over broken pots and panes of glass and old boxes turned upside down. She looked into every clump of weed, peered behind corners, and even looked up at the sun-warmed glass roofs where a cat might like to take a little nap.

"Tama, where are you?" she called until she was hoarse, but no black cat came bounding up to meet her. Keiko was soon past the last greenhouse, near the underpass beneath the freeway with its whizzing cars. She thought for one horrible moment what might have happened if Tama had somehow wandered up onto the freeway, but she brushed such a terrible idea aside as quickly as a cobweb. She turned at the last greenhouse and walked down the sidewalk that skirted Uncle Henry's property. It was all his fault for letting Tama out in the first place, she thought crossly, and for being allergic to Tama and giving her such a horrible bed. Keiko kicked at a stone and sent it flying down the sidewalk. When she looked up, she saw that she had almost hit Mike. He was riding an old black bike with his head held high, whistling "Yankee Doodle," and looking as though he owned the whole world. Behind him a big old hound loped along, his tail wagging, his tongue hanging out. Mike slowed down when he saw Keiko.

"Hey," he called. "What's the matter?"

"Tama's lost," Keiko said miserably. "What will I tell Auntie Kobe?"

Mike scratched his head. "Who're Tama and Auntie Kobe? And what're you carrying around that smelly fish for?" He held his nose and made a face. "P-U!" he said.

Keiko quickly hid the fish behind her back and then told Mike about Auntie Kobe and Jiro and about how they had hidden Tama on the ship all the way across the Pacific and how she belonged to her now, except that she was lost.

Mike straddled his bike, his dirty gray sneakers planted firmly on the sidewalk, his arms crossed over his chest. "How about that!" he said, looking impressed. "I lost a dog once."

"Did you find him?" Keiko asked.

Mike shook his head. "Nope, but Pop got King Arthur for me over at the Humane Society." Mike reached out to give King Arthur a pat on the head.

"Hey, I'll bet somebody found Tama and took her to the Humane Society," he said suddenly. "That's where she is, I'll bet."

Mike's enthusiasm was catching. "Do you think so?" Keiko asked. "Do you really?"

Mike was positive now. "Sure. I'll bet you anything that's where she is right now, chewing on a big fat old fishbone." He held his nose again and said, "Phew—ee! Even a cat wouldn't want that smelly ol' fish."

Keiko tried not to mind what Mike was saying about her dried fish. "Will you take me to the Humane Society to look for her?" she asked.

Mike backed away. "Who, me?" he asked. "Heck, no!"

"I could ride on the back of your bike," Keiko suggested. "I'm not very heavy."

Mike kept backing away inch by inch. "Me ride a girl on my bike?" he asked. "You're crazy!"

Keiko stood there feeling sorry for herself. "I'll never find Tama then," she said forlornly. "I'll probably never have another cat again in my whole entire life."

Keiko made Mike feel just bad enough to offer to go to the Humane Society himself. It was Saturday, and he really didn't have anything special to do until time for his paper route. "Aw, I'll go then," he said at last.

"But I'm going by myself. I'll go look for your ol' black cat."

"With yellow eyes and white paws and white on the tip of her tail," Keiko called after him. But Mike was already on his way. He was riding no hands now, and he whistled as he rode away.

Keiko felt better and ran the rest of the way home. When she got there, she saw Aunt Emi standing on the porch, looking worried.

"Oh, there you are, Kei-chan," she said. "I was beginning to worry about you. Do hurry. Auntie Kobe is going to San Francisco with us."

Keiko felt her heart flip over. "Did you tell her Tama was lost?" she asked.

"No, no, of course not," Aunt Emi said quickly. "Besides, I don't think she's lost at all. We'll leave a saucer of milk for her on the porch, and she'll probably be sitting there by the time we get back."

If she isn't, Mike will find her for me at the Humane Society, Keiko thought. But just to be on the safe side, Keiko took her dried fish out onto the porch and tied it to the railing with a piece of old string.

Then they got into Uncle Henry's car. Aunt Emi got in back and Keiko sat up in front because Aunt Emi said maybe Keiko could see more that way, and she'd sit in back and keep Auntie Kobe company.

Keiko sat up straight and still, looking out the window to the right and only glancing at Uncle Henry out of the corner of her eye from time to time. As they drove toward Oakland to get Auntie Kobe, Keiko could tell that Uncle Henry felt better today. For one thing, he had stopped sneezing, and for another, he had just sent a good shipment of carnations to the wholesaler in Chicago.

"They may double their Christmas order from us this year," he said, speaking of the wholesaler now. Keiko looked at him to show that she had heard, but Uncle Henry kept his eyes on the road and looked straight ahead. "If they keep expanding, they may double their orders for the rest of the year as well."

Aunt Emi sounded pleased. "How wonderful!" she said. "Maybe we'll be able to get that new automatic washer after all. And we'll start a college fund for you, Kei-chan, and get you some new books and clothes for school. You'll be going when the new term begins in February . . ." She was full of ideas, and it was hard for Keiko to be silent and sulk over Tama when Aunt Emi was so nice.

"Look," her aunt said now, pointing first to the right and then to the left as they drove through Oakland. "There's Lake Merritt, and that's the city hall over there, and the court house, and the library . . ."

Even Uncle Henry added words between Aunt

Emi's as he pointed out the duck feeding station and the playground and the boathouse, where you could rent rowboats to take out on the lake.

And then they were in front of Mrs. Fuji's gray house with its cracked and peeling paint, and Auntie Kobe came hurrying into the car, filling it with her talk and cheerful laugh.

She was so busy talking about the enormous baked ham Mrs. Fuji had made the night before that, much to Keiko's relief, she seemed to have forgotten all about Tama and didn't even ask how she was. And when she'd finished the ham, she talked of Jiro and how she had dreamed of him last night and how she had such a strong feeling that he was very near.

As Uncle Henry sped over the silver bridge that spanned the bay, Keiko closed her eyes against the glint of the sun on the water and tried hard to see if she couldn't have a feeling too—only about Tama. But all she saw were bright red and yellow spots flickering before her closed lids and the only feeling she had was the gurgle in her stomach. Keiko decided she just wasn't very good about having deep feelings about anything yet.

And it wasn't long before even Keiko herself stopped thinking about Tama, for now there was just too much to see all around. Uncle Henry took them first to Golden Gate Park, which turned out to be the biggest, greenest park Keiko had ever seen. It went on and on for what seemed like miles, and it even had an aquarium full of strange fish and a tea garden that looked like a garden in Kyoto. Keiko climbed the steep drum bridge and made a wish as she looked down into the pond, and she sat at the top of the stone steps that led to a temple gate and thought about the day her class had gone to Nikko for its spring excursion. Someone had gone off with her shoes from the hundreds of pairs lined up outside the shrine, and when she'd come out and not been able to find hers, her teacher, Miss Kawai, had gone to one of the souvenir shops and bought her a pair of wooden clogs. They were beautiful, with red velveteen thongs. Mother had sent some money with Keiko the very next day to pay for them, but Miss Kawai had said no, she wanted to give them to Keiko as a present. Keiko had never had a present from a teacher before, and she put the clogs away in a special box and never wanted to use them so they would last forever. She knew even now just where she had left them in her closet, warning Hana that she must never, never borrow them. Keiko sat there thinking about Miss Kawai, and Nikko and Mother and Hiro and Hana and everybody back home when Aunt Emi called her.

"Come along, Kei-chan," she said. "There's lots

more to see in San Francisco," and she came over and took her hand, just as Mother used to do when she was a little girl.

They went next to see the sea lions stretched out on the big brown ocean-sprayed rock near the Cliff House. Keiko could smell again the familiar salt spray of the ocean, and Auntie Kobe began to talk about the Nikko Maru and Captain Sawada and the night of the sukiyaki party when she had fainted.

"Mah, but those officers were all nice," Auntie Kobe said. "I almost wish I were back on that beautiful green ship again."

Before Auntie Kobe could grow too homesick, Uncle Henry hurried them on to the zoo and then to Fisherman's Wharf with its fleet of crab boats and the vendors who sold crab from steaming cauldrons right out on the sidewalk. They ate in a restaurant with windows that looked out over the wharf, and it was only when Keiko saw a plate of broiled trout go by that she thought of Tama and wondered if by now she were back nibbling at the fish on the railing. And then, as though Auntie Kobe could read her mind, she suddenly turned and asked Keiko how Tama was getting along.

Keiko wanted to crawl right under the table. She just couldn't bear to tell Auntie Kobe she had lost her beautiful Tama on the very first day she'd had her. And then Aunt Emi came to her rescue.

"Why, Tama's fine," she said brightly. "She's been out exploring the neighborhood, and by now she's probably found some fine new friends."

Auntie Kobe smiled and looked pleased. "I just knew Tama would be happy living with Kei-chan," she said. "I knew I had decided to do the right thing."

Keiko looked down at her lap and twisted her napkin. Aunt Emi coughed gently, and Uncle Henry sneezed as though the very thought of Tama were too much for him. Only Auntie Kobe went right on eating her fresh crab as though she hadn't a worry in the world.

When it was time to go home, they took the ferry back to the Oakland pier, and Keiko went all over the ship looking into people's faces to see if she might not find a Japanese man, about forty, with a scar down his cheek. She would feel a little better about having lost Tama if she could make up for it by finding Jiro. But even though Auntie Kobe had felt that Jiro was very close, he wasn't so close that he was on the same ferryboat.

They took Auntie Kobe back to Mrs. Fuji's peeling gray house, and when they got back home to Rich-

mond, there was Mike sitting on the front steps waiting for them. He held an enormous cardboard carton
on his lap, and he was reading a comic book. Keiko
took one look at the carton and raced out of the car.
"Mike, you found her!" she shouted.

"Wait'll you see what I found," Mike said, getting
to his feet.

Aunt Emi invited him inside. "What in the world
have you got in that carton?" she asked. "It looks so
heavy."

"Yes, ma'am," Mike puffed. "It *is* heavy." And picking it up with a great deal of effort, he started inside.

"Wait a minute," Uncle Henry called. "I'll give you
a hand."

But Mike had already staggered into the house with
his carton, and just as he got inside, he tripped on the
rug and fell sprawling to the floor. As he fell, he
dropped his box, the flaps flew open, and from inside
jumped not one black cat, but three! They leaped out
with frightened yowls and then proceeded to run in
different directions all over the house.

"Stop!" Keiko shouted, but the cats spread like
black ink. One ran into the bedroom and hid under
the bed; the second ran into the kitchen and leaped to
the top of the china cabinet; the third scrambled up
the drapes in the living room and perched on the cur-

tain rod, glaring at everybody like a small black pan-
ther.

"I couldn't tell which was Tama," Mike explained
hopelessly, "so I brought all three of them back." He
reached into his pocket and pulled out a turtle with its
back painted yellow. "I got me a turtle, too," he said
proudly, but Aunt Emi asked him to please put it
away and help catch the cats.

Keiko ran into the kitchen first and stared up at the
cat on the cabinet. "You're not Tama at all," she said
dismally, "but you'd better come down anyway."

The cat just looked at her with its yellow-green eyes
and twitched its black tail. Keiko got up on a chair,
reached up toward the cat, and knocked Uncle
Henry's coffee cup into the sink with a crash. Now
Mike chased the second cat into the kitchen too, where
it ran under the stove and glared at him like a black
witch. "Hissssss," it said wickedly.

"Darned cat!" Mike muttered, and he dived under
the stove, grabbed the struggling cat, and shouted,
"Hey, if this isn't Tama, open the door. Quick!"

It wasn't Tama and Keiko opened the door.

"Darn ol' cat," Mike muttered again, and he
watched as it leaped away down the steps.

Aunt Emi hurried into the kitchen with a broom,
which she shook at the cat up on the cabinet. "Come
down this instant," she demanded, and she waved the

broom in the cat's face until it leaped onto the table, where Mike caught it at last.

"Out you go too," he said, and he shooed it out the back door.

Now there was only the cat sitting on the curtain rod in the living room. Uncle Henry glared at it as he moved all the breakable things from the tables nearby.

"I'll make her move," Mike said, and leaping and clapping his hands at the cat, he shouted, "Scat!"

The cat moved, all right. It landed right on the mantel and crouched beside the dancing doll in the glass case.

"Oh, don't let her break that," Aunt Emi said frantically. "Somebody do something!"

While the cat glared at Mike, Uncle Henry tiptoed quietly from behind, made a quick snatch, and finally got the screeching, scratching cat out of the house. By the time he closed the door, he was rubbing his eyes and sneezing again.

"I'll be glad if I never see another cat in this house again," he said gloomily, and he blew his nose and marched out of the room.

"All that trouble for nothing," Mike said miserably.

"And Uncle Henry still hates cats," Keiko added dismally.

She sighed and went out to look at the back porch. The milk was still in the saucer and the fish hung limply on the railing. They were right back where they had started in the morning, except that now Mike had a pet turtle.

"I'm going to call him Herbert," he said, "after my shop teacher." And he put it in his pocket and went home.

REGGIE'S NO-GOOD BIRD

by Nellie Burchardt

The three o'clock bell clanged inside the school on First Avenue. Almost at once the boys of Mrs. Sullivan's fourth grade, which was nearest the door, burst out onto the sidewalk. As usual, Reggie Thompson was in the lead. He blinked, and shaded his eyes with his hand as he came out into the dazzling June sunlight.

"Hey, Reggie," yelled a boy behind him. Reggie

turned his head just in time to be hit in the face with a baseball cap.

"I'll get you for that, Joey," he yelled.

He snatched the cap from the ground and flung it back at Joey. Joey ducked when he saw it coming, and the cap hit a girl behind him.

She shrieked. "You awful Reggie Thompson! I'm going to tell Mrs. Sullivan on you."

"I should worry, I should care," chanted Reggie. "Come on, Joey. Last one to the corner is teacher's pet."

The two boys raced off.

At the corner, the sixth-grade crossing guard stood on the curb. His arms were outspread to keep anyone from crossing the busy street before the light changed, but Reggie was going too fast to stop in time. He ran full force into the guard's back.

"Okay. Who's the wise guy?" the boy demanded as he turned around. His face was flushed with anger. "Oh, it's *you* again," he said as he caught sight of Reggie. "I warned you the last time, if you got funny just once more, I'd report you. Now, what's your name?" He grabbed a handful of Reggie's shirt.

"Puddintane," jeered Reggie.

"*Very* funny. What's your real name?"

The light changed and the heavy traffic screeched to

a halt. The stream of children following Reggie divided and went around him and the guard, who glanced around to be sure the street was safe to cross. In that instant, Reggie yanked away from his hold and dashed across to the other side.

"Hey, you, come back here," shouted the guard. "I didn't say you could go."

But Reggie was lost in the crowd of children. Joey caught up with him.

"Boy! Are you going to be in trouble!" said Joey.

"Aw, he's too bossy. He thinks he knows it all just because he's a sixth grader," grumbled Reggie. "I didn't mean to bump into him. I just couldn't stop in time. Why should he report me for that?"

"He'll get you the next time he sees you, anyhow," said Joey.

"You're a big help," said Reggie.

Three other boys came running across the street to join Reggie and Joey.

"What'll we do today, Reg?" one of the boys asked.

"How about seeing what we can find in those buildings they're tearing down? My brother found some real good junk there the other day," said Reggie.

"Yeah!"

"Great!"

"Let's go!"

The boys tore off at top speed along the crowded sidewalk. A group of girls scattered before them with little shrieks.

"It's that awful Reggie Thompson," said one of the girls.

"He's the worst pest in the whole school," another added.

By now, Reggie and his friends had reached the next block. Down at the other end a big metal ball swung back and forth from a crane as the wreckers turned the buildings into piles of rubble. At this end of the block the houses were still standing, with all their windows marked by big white X's.

Reggie grabbed a broken brick from the sidewalk and heaved it at a window. The glass gave a satisfying crash that could be heard even over the roar of the traffic.

"Ya-ay!" yelled Reggie. "Bull's-eye!"

"Anyone can hit a target that big," said Joey. He picked up another brick and was just about to throw it when a man's head appeared in the broken window.

The man shook his fist at the boys. "Go on. Get out of here," he shouted.

Joey dropped the brick and ran.

"How do you like that?" said Reggie. "They've got a watchman for this dump. A guy can't have any fun at all around here."

He ran after Joey, leaving the other boys behind.
"Joey, wait," he yelled.

In the next block they slowed down.

"What'll we do now?" asked Joey.

Across the street was the City Housing Project
where they both lived. They started to take a shortcut
through the playground.

At the entrance was a sign that read,

NO
Ball Playing
Roller Skating
Bicycle Riding
Dogs

Reggie read the sign out loud. "How do they expect
a guy to live around here?" he grumbled. "It's a wonder they don't make a rule against breathing."

"Yeah," agreed Joey. "What do they want us to do?
Play with dolls like girls? Or play in the sandbox with
the little kids there?"

They hurried past the sandbox. The nearby benches
were lined solidly with mothers, keeping an eye on
their younger children.

Reggie nudged Joey in the ribs. He pointed at the
benches filled with women. "Look, Joey," he said,
"wall-to-wall mothers!"

Joey grinned and kicked a stone. Both boys ran after

it as it rolled along. When it came to a stop, Reggie beat Joey to the next kick. Then he ran after the stone and picked it up before Joey could reach it.

A lamppost with its tempting round light globe stood nearby.

"Bet I can hit that light," said Reggie.

"In broad daylight? You're asking for trouble," said Joey. "The maintenance will catch you."

"Aw, I can run faster than they can," boasted Reggie. He let the rock fly.

"Missed by a mile," taunted Joey. "You've got an eye like a dead eagle."

"Oh, yeah?" said Reggie. "My fingers just slipped."

Beyond the playground was Reggie's building, and there the project trees began—the only trees within blocks. In one of them was a nestful of blue jay fledglings. Two of them had just pulled themselves up to the edge of the nest, where they teetered and clutched the rim fearfully with their still-weak claws. They stretched their half-grown wings. It would still be some time before they were strong enough to fly.

"I'll bet I can hit that no-good old blue jay there," said Reggie. "I'll bet I won't miss this time."

As there was no stone handy, he picked up a crushed tin can lying beside a wastebasket, and threw it at the birds.

"Missed," shrieked Joey. "Is your aim rotten today!"

One baby jay fluttered unsteadily back into the nest. The other one flapped its wings wildly, then lost its balance and fell to the ground.

Several girls walking behind the boys screamed.

"Ha!" said Reggie. "I did not miss. I got him, all right, all right."

The bird lay on the ground at the base of the tree, its eyes closed.

"I got him. I got him," gloated Reggie. He did a triumphant hunter's dance around the trunk of the tree.

"Aw-w-w. It's a *baby* bird," cried one of the girls.

"Reggie Thompson, you're the meanest boy in the whole school," said another.

It was that Silly Diane from his class, Reggie noticed. She was always screaming. He couldn't stand her.

He stopped prancing around the tree. "I sure am," he said, grinning proudly. "And I've got the best aim in the whole school, too," he boasted.

"Is the bird dead?" asked Diane.

Reggie shrugged. "I guess so," he said.

"Why don't you find out?" asked Diane.

Reggie looked at her.

"How?" he asked.

"Why don't you pick it up?"

Reggie nudged the jay with the toe of his sneaker. The bird's eyes remained closed.

"He's dead, all right," said Reggie.

"How can you be sure, unless you pick it up?" asked Diane.

Reggie hesitated. He had never touched anything dead before—except bugs and worms, and they didn't count.

"You're scared to touch it," said Diane.

"I am not."

"You are too. I dare you to pick it up."

Reggie bent down and gingerly scooped up the bird in his hands. Its head wobbled loosely on its neck.

Reggie shifted one hand to keep the bird's neck steady. Its body felt warm in his hands. Dark-gray feathers were just breaking out of their sheaths on the bird's chest, and the bright-blue tail feathers with clear white adult markings were partly grown out.

The jay lifted its head weakly for a fraction of an inch. Its eyes remained closed.

Reggie was so shocked when it moved that he almost dropped it.

"It's alive! It's alive!" screamed Diane in his ear.

He winced. "It's alive," he repeated in amazement.

The bird's head sank down onto his hand again. Suddenly Reggie felt sick to his stomach. Up until now he hadn't thought of the bird as something alive. It had been only a target up in a tree.

"What are you going to do with it now?" asked Diane.

"Maybe put it back in the nest," said Reggie, looking up and measuring the climb to the limb that held the nest.

"Do you think the mother will know how to take care of it when it's hurt like that?" asked Diane.

"How should I know?" asked Reggie. He was feeling sicker by the minute. Holding this warm bird was a lot different from picking up dead bugs.

The bird raised its head again. This time it tried to open its eyes. Reggie could see its sides heaving up and down with the effort of breathing.

"You've got to do something about it," said Diane. "It'll be your fault if it dies."

Suddenly Reggie wished he had never heard of tin cans or blue jays—or girls either, for that matter. Why did the silly girls have to make such a fuss over an old blue jay? Blue jays were no good anyhow. Reggie had heard his father say so time and again. "Noisy, thieving, no-good varmints," his father called them. He had lived on a farm when he was a boy, and he ought to know.

"Well, what are you going to do about it?" asked Diane.

Reggie looked around for help from Joey, but Joey had disappeared. A fine pal he was.

"Oh, leave me alone," he muttered. Now he was almost sure he was going to be sick.

"I'll take it home and take care of it," said Diane, reaching out her hand for the bird.

He'd like to see her take care of anything, Reggie thought. Every time she saw a bug she squealed.

"You keep your hands off him. He's my bird," he said.

He undid the two top buttons of his shirt and tucked the bird inside.

"What are you going to do with it?" asked Diane.

"Mind your own business," said Reggie. He took a threatening step toward her.

"You leave me alone, Reginald Thompson," she said, backing uneasily toward the other girls.

Reggie turned and started to walk away. He could feel the girls staring after him. He heard footsteps behind him. Quickly he spun around. Diane squealed and almost fell over backward.

"Don't you touch me, Reginald Thompson. Don't you dare!" she screeched.

"Who's touching you?" asked Reggie.

He turned and went up the walk toward his own building. This time the girls did not follow him.

He felt the bird stir inside his shirt. Now what on earth had he taken the bird for and what was he going to do with it? he wondered. He didn't even know what to feed a blue jay. He just knew he wasn't going to let any girl have his bird.

Reggie found Joey waiting for him in the hallway of their building.

"A fine pal you are," he said, "leaving me with all those girls."

"I thought you were right behind me," Joey answered. "Why did you stay there talking to them?"

"You don't think I was going to let them get my bird, do you?" asked Reggie.

"What's the difference? It's dead, isn't it?"

"No."

"It looked dead to me. What did you do with it?"

"I've got it here inside my shirt."

"You're kidding! What do you want to keep it for?"

"Because—" Reggie couldn't have explained it. He just knew that the bird was his now.

He got the apartment key from Mrs. Lomax next

door, as he always did. His mother would not be home from work until five o'clock.

"Sh-h-h!" he warned Joey as he unlocked the door. "Pop's asleep."

"Is he on night shift again?"

Reggie nodded. The boys tiptoed back to the room Reggie shared with his big brother Hank. There Reggie took out the bird and laid it carefully on his bed.

The jay seemed to be breathing a little more easily, but its eyes were still closed.

"He doesn't look so good," said Joey.

Reggie knelt down beside the bed and looked at the bird closely. Joey was looking right over his shoulder. It made Reggie nervous.

"Give me room, will you?" he said.

Joey backed up a step. "Is he hurt bad?" he asked.

"No, he's just stunned from the fall," said Reggie, trying to sound more sure of himself than he really felt.

"I think I'll get him some water," he said, getting to his feet again.

"How's he going to drink it when he's unconscious?" asked Joey. "That's dumb."

"Not to drink, stupid. To put on his head. Don't you know that's what they do with people when they faint?" said Reggie. Who did Joey think he was, telling him how to take care of his own bird?

Reggie went into the bathroom and got a glassful of water.

A sleepy voice came from behind the closed door of his parents' room. "That you, Reg?"

"Yes, Pop." His father mustn't see the bird. Reggie knew well enough what his father thought of blue jays. Pop would make him get rid of it, for sure.

"What are you doing, Reg?" came his father's sleepy voice again.

"Nothing, Pop."

"Well—do it more quietly."

"All right, Pop."

Reggie tiptoed back to his room with the glass of water. The bird still lay motionless on the bed.

Joey watched as Reggie dipped up a few drops of water with his fingertips and sprinkled them on the bird's head. The blue jay stirred slightly.

"Hey, how about that!" exclaimed Joey. "It worked. He's coming to." He looked at Reggie in surprise.

"Nothing to it," said Reggie. "Didn't I tell you I knew what to do? I've been thinking of being a doctor when I grow up." He hadn't been thinking of it for more than ten seconds, but there was no need to tell Joey that.

"You?" said Joey. "With your marks? That's a laugh."

Reggie ignored him. What was the matter with

everyone? No one—not even his own best pal—gave him credit for being able to do anything. He'd show Joey. He'd get this bird well if it was the last thing he did.

Now the jay's beak was slightly open, and Reggie held a drop of water on his forefinger and let it drip into the bird's mouth. The jay closed his beak and tilted its head up a bit. It seemed to be considering the taste of the water. Then its beak opened a shade wider than before.

"Will you look at that?" said Joey. "He wants more."

Reggie let another drop of water run into the bird's beak. Again the jay tilted its head up.

"Do you think he can swallow?" asked Joey.

"It just runs down his throat when he raises his head," said Reggie.

"Since when are you such an expert on birds?" asked Joey.

"Didn't you ever watch pigeons? Don't you know anything?" asked Reggie.

Joey was silent.

There was a noise at the front door.

"That must be Hank already," said Reggie. "I didn't think he'd be home yet from delivering his papers. Quick! We've got to hide the bird."

"How about this?" asked Joey. He picked up Reggie's pajama top from the floor where Reggie had dropped it that morning.

"It'll have to do," said Reggie. He spread the pajama top carefully over the bird.

His big brother came into the room, went straight to his own bed, and flung himself down onto it without a word.

"Hi," said Reggie.

Hank looked over at the two younger boys in surprise.

"Hi, infants," he said. "I didn't see you sitting there on the floor." He closed his eyes and sighed. "If anyone ever offers you a paper route," he added, "just laugh in his face."

"Hard work, huh?" said Reggie, trying to put a lot of sympathy into his voice. Maybe if he put Hank in a good mood, he wouldn't object to the bird.

Hank opened his eyes and looked sharply at Reggie. "How come you're so sympathetic all of a sudden?" he asked.

Reggie looked down. Hank always saw through him. The trouble was, whatever age Reggie was, Hank had been there first and knew all the tricks.

Hank rose on one elbow. "What have you got there?" he asked.

"Got? Where?" asked Reggie innocently.

"There on your bed. What are you trying to hide?"

"Hide? We're not hiding anything, are we, Joey?" said Reggie.

"Uh-uh," said Joey.

"Oh, yes, you are," said Hank. "What's on your bed there?"

"That? Oh, that's just my pajamas. I forgot to hang them up this morning."

"What's under them?"

"Nothing," said Reggie, trying to get between Hank and the pajama top.

"Come on, infant," said Hank. "Let me see what you've got."

Reggie gave up, afraid that Hank might try to grab the pajama top and in doing so would hurt the bird.

"It's just a blue jay," he said lifting the covering.

"For Pete's sake!" exclaimed Hank. "What'll you drag home next?" He stood up and came over to Reggie's bed to look at the bird more closely. "What do you want with a dead bird? Don't you know they're full of germs and stuff? Maybe he died of rabies."

"He's not dead," said Reggie.

"Well, if he isn't now, he's going to be soon," said Hank. "And you'd better get him out of my room."

"It's my room too. And he's not going to die!" exclaimed Reggie.

Suddenly the bird's living seemed the most important thing in all the world. If it lived, that decided it.

He'd be a doctor when he grew up—maybe a famous surgeon. Then they'd all laugh out of the other side of their faces—Diane and Joey and Hank and all of them.

"Pipe down," warned Hank. "You'll wake up Pop."

"He's *not* going to die," repeated Reggie in a softer voice. "He's better already."

As if to back up his words, the jay lifted its head.

Hank looked at the bird in disgust. "What do you want with a no-good old blue jay, anyhow?" he asked. "All they ever do is squawk."

That was just like Hank, thought Reggie—always running down anything that belonged to him.

"Don't you dare call him no-good!" Reggie clenched his fists in rage, forgetting that he had been calling blue jays the same thing only a short while before. "He's just as good as the dumb old turtle you had last year."

"Okay—okay!" said Hank. "Keep your shirt on! But you'd better not let Mom or Pop see him."

"You won't tell them, will you, Hank?" asked Reggie.

"That all depends," said Hank.

"On what?" asked Reggie uneasily.

"On a lot of things," said Hank, sitting down on his own bed again and looking thoughtfully at Reggie. "What's it worth to you?"

"What do you mean?" asked Reggie.

As if he didn't know. That Hank was the kind of fellow who wouldn't give you his old chewing gum wrappers for nothing.

"If I do you a favor, what will you do for me?" asked Hank.

"I don't know," said Reggie.

"Let me see now," said Hank. "That idea has some extremely interesting possibilities." He leaned back on the bed again, with his arms clasped behind his head, and looked up at the ceiling with a pleased smile.

"Now—you might make my bed for me every morning—or polish my shoes every day. No, those aren't things I really *have* to do. I've got it!" Hank sat up straight again. "My paper route! It's too long and takes up too much of my time. You can help me with it. And if you don't make any mistakes, I just *might* consider keeping quiet about the bird. Though why anyone would want to keep a no-good bird like that, I can't imagine."

"That's not fair," exclaimed Reggie. "Why should I do your work for you?"

"Oh, well," said Hank, "if you're not interested, I'll have to speak to Mom about it when she gets home. I think she might like to know how the bird got hurt, too. Mothers don't approve of that sort of thing, you know."

"How did you know I—" Reggie started to speak before he realized Hank had trapped him.

"Ah-ha!" said Hank. "Got you that time! Now I think you'll be interested in those papers, won't you?"

"Oh—all right—I guess so," said Reggie.

"What do you mean, you *guess* so?" asked Hank. "You'd just better be sure."

"All right. I'm sure."

Behind Reggie, the bird gave a faint peep. Reggie hurried back to look at his patient.

It stretched out its neck and opened its beak wide, making a bright-pink diamond shape.

"Peep!" said the bird again, more firmly.

"Look! He's okay now!" exclaimed Joey.

"Maybe he's hungry," said Reggie.

"Maybe he thinks you're his father," said Joey.

"Why would he think a dumb thing like that?"

"All right. He thinks you're his mother then," said Hank.

"Ha-ha!" said Reggie. "Aren't we funny today!"

"Watch your lip, junior," said Hank, "or somebody might just happen to hear about that bird."

"What do you suppose he eats?" asked Reggie, quickly changing the subject.

"Birdseed or bugs, I guess," said Joey. "My grandmother's canary eats birdseed and lettuce."

"But he's not a canary," said Reggie. "Maybe what a canary eats would make him sick."

"All I can say is you'd better feed him soon and shut him up, or he won't be a secret any longer," said Hank.

Now the bird was keeping up a steady "peep—peep —peep."

"But where am I going to get something to feed him?" said Reggie.

"Why don't you ask Mrs. Lomax's canary to lend you some birdseed?" asked Hank.

"It's worth trying, at least," answered Reggie.

He went next door and begged some birdseed from Mrs. Lomax. But when he put some in a little dish in front of the bird, it kept on peeping. Reggie tried pushing its head down into the dish, but the bird struggled to get free, and peeped louder. Even dropping the seed into the bird's wide-open mouth did not work. The jay merely let the seed roll out of the side of its beak.

"Maybe he's too young for birdseed," said Reggie at last. "How am I going to find out what to feed him?"

"They invented something for people like you," said Hank.

"What?"

"Libraries."

"Of course! Sometimes I think you're a genius, Hank!" exclaimed Reggie.

"Well, not quite, but I'm getting there," answered Hank. "I'm glad you noticed, though."

"Oh—shut up!" Reggie knelt down and fished an old shoe box from under his bed. He dumped out the collection of marbles, baseball cards, and string that it contained, and put the bird in it. Terrified, the jay threshed around, banging its wings against the hard sides of the box.

"He's going to hurt himself that way," said Joey.

Reggie picked up the bird again, stuffed his pajama top into the box, then put the bird back. It settled down and seemed to be more comfortable.

"Come on, Joey," said Reggie. "Let's hurry before Charley starts peeping again."

"Charley, is it?" said Hank. "What makes you so sure it's a 'he'?"

"Of course it's a 'he,' " said Reggie. "You don't think I'd have any old *girl* bird, do you?"

THE SPIDER PLANT

by Yetta Speevack

Carmen Santos, her brother Pedro, and their mother were sad to leave Puerto Rico, but glad Papá had found a job in New York and an apartment where they could join him.

The one thing Carmen found she never really did get used to was the lack of trees and flowers and bushes in New York. And when the weather got cold, colder than Carmen had ever dreamed it could get, everything seemed very bleak. Sometimes she and the other girls walked down to the big flower market near their house and looked inside at the bright flowers. That helped a little, but it was not the same. And when the weather got very cold, being outside was not much fun.

So Carmen tried harder and harder to get the plant-watering job at school. Many times she did. But sometimes the teacher said, "We must take turns. You've had the plant job too often."

Then Carmen would beg, "Please, please, just once more."

"Well, all right," Miss Hall would often say. "But just this once."

When it was her job, Carmen took good care of the plants. Every day she looked for new green shoots. She washed the leaves and turned the plants so that the sun and light would hit every side. One day in January, when she was loosening the soil around the spider plant, she looked up to see Miss Hall watching her.

"Have you joined the garden club yet, Carmen?" she asked.

Carmen turned in surprise. "Is there a garden club?" she asked.

"Didn't anyone tell you about it?" said Miss Hall. "I thought I had myself. It meets on Friday after school. Mr. Janitz, the science teacher, is in charge of it. I'm sure he'd like to have you. Ask your mother if you can't stay on Friday, and I'll speak to Mr. Janitz about you. The club sponsors a school flower show in June."

Carmen could hardly believe what she had heard. How could she not have known? How wonderful to have a garden club!

Later that morning Miss Hall said to the class, "Why don't we make a plant for Carmen to take home? Our spider plant has a great many new green shoots. Carmen deserves one for taking such good care of all the plants."

"Oh, how nice," said Carmen. "That is my second nice surprise today." Then she remembered the apartment. "But we have no sunny windows. I can't have a plant at home."

Miss Hall explained that spider plants do not need much light. "The plant will do well under a lamp," she said.

That afternoon Carmen chose a little shoot from the big plant. She set the baby plant in the middle of a pot and added soil to make it stand up straight. Finally she gave her plant some water. She could hardly wait to take it home.

"I hope your little plant does well so you can enter it in the flower show," Miss Hall called after her as she left school that afternoon. Carmen was in such a hurry she did not even wait for Iris. She ran all the way home and up the three flights of stairs.

"Mamá, Mamá," she called.

Her mother opened the door quickly *"Qué pasó? What happened? Is somebody chasing you?"*

"Mira, look what I have."

"Where did you get the plant?"

"My teacher let me make it from one of her plants, because I take good care of the plants in school. Now I'll have a plant for the flower show that the garden club has in June. And, Mamá, there's a garden club at school that meets on Friday afternoons. Can I go?"

Mamá held up her hands and laughed. "One thing at a time, *niña,"* she said. "One thing at a time.

"First of all, where will you keep your plant? We haven't enough light in this apartment for a plant." Mamá sighed, and Carmen was surprised to see the sad look that passed over her face. But she quickly smiled again as she reached out and touched a leaf of the little spider plant.

"This plant doesn't need a window," Carmen explained. "My teacher says it will do well under an electric light."

"Well, I hope it grows here," said Mamá softly. "And now about the garden club. What about that?"

Carmen explained, and Mamá was almost as happy

as Carmen about it. "What a good thing," she said. "You can learn much, and maybe someday we will have a garden again." Then she went out to the kitchen to begin supper, and Carmen began to look for a place for her plant.

She looked first in the living room. The table was the only flat space large enough for it. But if she put it there, what would happen when she had to set the table for meals? And then, too, the light was high up in the ceiling, too far away to do the plant much good.

Carmen went to the small kitchen. She looked at the ledge over the sink.

"Not in here, *chiquita*," said her mother, guessing her thoughts. "When the stove is on, it gets too hot in this little kitchen."

Carmen went on to her room. In it, there was only a bed, one chair, and a small chest of drawers. She had to keep her schoolbooks and other things like that on top of the chest. Besides, the light was not good. There was a small window way up high that looked out on a court, but she had to climb on her bed to get to it. And it didn't let in much light anyway. No, her room would not be good. She was standing there holding her plant when she thought of Pedro's fish tank with its light to keep the fish warm. Just the place! She went into the living room, moved Pedro's fish tank over, and put her little spider plant under the light.

She went to help Mamá then, and she had almost forgotten what she had done when Pedro came home. He had been at Mr. Rocano's. When he came in the door, he went right to his fish tank. Carmen heard him do this, but she did not think anything of it. It was what he always did.

"Who did this?" she heard him call in his loud, grown-up voice. Only then did she remember the plant. She ran to the living room.

"It's my plant. Miss Hall gave it to me. And I want it to have some light, too."

"Not here, silly. Do you want one side of my tank to be hot and the other cold? If you need light, get your own lamp," he shouted.

Carmen took her plant off the table, but she was angry at Pedro. How could she get a job and buy her own lamp when she had to help her mother clean house on Saturdays? Pedro didn't seem to remember that girls had to help at home, and boys didn't. Pedro cared more for his fish than for her, just as she had suspected.

She carried the plant back to her room. Piling her books to one side, she set the pot on the small chest of drawers, which stood against the dark wall.

On Friday, Carmen went to the garden club. When she came home, she ran to look at her plant. There was no question about it, it was drooping. She quickly washed the leaves and watered the soil. But the plant did not look well, even so. It needed light, and she must find a way to give it some.

"Where's Pedro?" Carmen asked Mamá. She would beg Pedro to let her plant stand under his lamp for just ten minutes.

"He's working for Mr. Rocano again today," Mamá answered.

Here was a chance to give her plant some light. It wouldn't hurt Pedro's fish; he wouldn't even have to know about it. The plant would be gone from the tank long before he got home. She pushed the tank over to one side of the table again and put the spider plant directly under the lamp.

Just then the door bell rang, and Mrs. Morales came in to ask Carmen to sit with María while she went to the store to get some milk and bread.

"May I go, Mamá?" asked Carmen.

"The baby loves Carmen," said Mrs. Morales. "Carmen should be a teacher when she grows up. She has taught María to clap hands, wave good-by, and point to her ears, mouth, and eyes."

"I hope Carmen will be a teacher someday," said Mamá, smiling happily.

Carmen went off with Mrs. Morales to the apartment next door. She sat with María until almost five o'clock, because Mrs. Morales did not return as quickly as she had promised. She met an old friend from Aquadilla, her hometown in Puerto Rico, and did not realize how long they talked.

When Carmen left the Morales apartment to go into her own house, Pedro was coming up the stairs. Carmen saw him and remembered her plant. But it was too late. Inside, Pedro hurried over to his fish tank. He didn't even remove his leather jacket.

"No, not again!" he shrieked. "Mamá, come here." Mamá hurried into the living room. "Look at my tank! It's lucky it didn't fall off the table and break. Well, I warned her." And before Carmen or her mother had a chance to grab the plant, he smacked it off the table.

The pot broke into a thousand pieces. Carmen was so surprised she couldn't open her mouth to speak. What would she tell her teacher? And what was the point of belonging to a garden club when she had no plant at all? And what about the plant? It meant as much to her as Pedro's fish meant to him. And now it was gone.

Carmen ran to her bedroom. She shut the door, threw herself on the bed, and buried her head in the pillow. She didn't even cry. And she didn't answer her mother when she called.

Soon Carmen heard Papá come home from work.

She heard him talking first to Mamá and then to Pedro. And after a while he called her.

"Come, Carmen. Come to the table. Supper is ready."

Carmen didn't feel like eating. But Papá had called, and she knew that in the Santos house when Papá called she must obey.

"Look, Carmen," said Papá, when she came to the table, "only the little pot is broken. The plant is still good. Put your plant in the little rooster sugar bowl. Mamá says you like it."

Carmen nodded. She still had no voice.

After supper, Mamá watched as Carmen put some of the broken pieces of the flower pot at the bottom of the sugar bowl. She had seen her teacher do that to pots that didn't have a hole at the bottom for drainage. Then Carmen filled the bottom of the bowl with some of the earth her mother had picked up from the floor.

Her father, coming over to the table, saw her set the little plant in the middle and gently press the earth around it.

"You don't have enough soil," he said. "Go to the five and ten cent store tomorrow and buy a small bag. I'll give you the money."

"I'll buy you a watering can," said Mamá.

"I'll buy you a little lamp," said Pedro, not looking into her eyes.

It was just like a birthday, with presents all around.

Carmen held the little plant in her hand and smiled at all of them. "Soon it will bloom, my spider plant," she said. "And the little white flower will be a 'thank you' to all of you."

Papá's face grew serious. "Our family was like your plant, Carmen. We lost our home in Puerto Rico but not our courage and strength. Our family is still whole."

A WONDERFUL, TERRIBLE TIME

by Mary Stolz

Summer.

The sun was so hot, so bright, that shade had no-where to go except in the alleys with the trash cans and the cats and the clothes hanging slack on the lines.

Mady Guthrie and Sue Ellen Forrest sat on the stoop in front of their apartment building and watched boys kill one another in the street.

"Bang, bang, bang!"

A boy screamed, staggered, fell to the ground. Then he jumped to his feet, aimed a finger at his assassin.

"Bang, bang! Bang, bang, bang!"

"You're dead."

"Now you're dead!"

They killed up and down the street, on the sidewalks, on the steps of buildings, in and out of the alleys.

Bang, bang, bang, bang! They filled the summer air with invisible bullets that never missed their mark.

Sue Ellen and Mady watched, yawning.

A cat walked by, sat down, and watched them. Then it too yawned and walked into the alley to be cool where the shade was.

Their last year's teacher, Miss Rice, came down the street. She carried a rose-colored umbrella against the sun and looked different from her classroom self.

"Hi, teach," said Mady and Sue Ellen together.

Miss Rice looked at them and took a second to remember who they were. Then she said, "Sue Ellen. Mady. How are you? What are you doing?"

"Nothing."

"Can't you think of something to do?"

"We will," said Sue Ellen.

"Later," said Mady.

Miss Rice walked on. She had been a pretty good

teacher, the kind who could keep a whole class in its seat when the lesson was going on. She did it just with a look. In some classes the kids wandered all around and the teacher didn't know what to do about it. But Miss Rice just looked, and all the children stayed where they belonged and learned something.

Just the same, a new teacher lay ahead now, and Miss Rice was out of their lives. Sue Ellen and Mady forgot her as she rounded the corner.

"Let's play hopscotch," said Sue Ellen.

There was an old blue hopscotch game, almost wiped out, on the sidewalk in front of them. They had drawn it themselves, in blue chalk, days ago. It was almost gone from feet walking on it but was still clear enough to see.

They played, hopping from box to box, using a bunch of safety pins for throwing.

"It's too hot," Sue Ellen decided after a while.

"Okay," said Mady.

They sat on the stoop again, watching the boys, who never seemed to get too hot to kill one another.

Down at the end of the block a fireman appeared. As soon as he came, children gathered like flies around a melon. Some of them already had bathing suits on, as if they'd known he was going to come and put the sprinkler on the hydrant for children to splash.

"Oh, boy," said Sue Ellen. "Let's play in the water."

"We don't have any bathing suits."

"We'll wear old shorts and shirts. We'll ask my momma."

Mady's mother worked. She was a nurse at a nearby hospital. But Sue Ellen's mother stayed home and kept house. Sue Ellen's father was a taxi driver. Mady's father was dead.

They ran upstairs into Sue Ellen's apartment, where Mrs. Forrest was ironing clothes, wiping the sweat off her forehead.

"Whew," she said cheerfully, as the girls burst through the door. "What a job. You know, one day you'll go through that door without opening it. Then we'll have to pay to get a new one."

"Can we put on old shorts and shirts and play in the fire hydrant?" Sue Ellen shouted. "The fireman just opened it. It's only half an hour, Momma. They only leave it open half an hour."

"Has he got the sprinkler on it?"

"Oh, yes. Can we?"

"Well, I don't know."

"Oh, boy, thanks," said Sue Ellen and tore into the bedroom. Mady followed.

"She didn't say Yes."

"She said 'I don't know.' You know that means Yes.

If she means No she says 'No,' or 'Ask your father.' You go get your things on too."

Mady had two keys to her apartment, which was just across the hall. You had to open the door twice. Once with the key to the old lock, and once with the key to the bolt her mother had had put on. Mrs. Guthrie said roughneck elements ruled the neighborhood. She said that Mrs. Forrest, who sometimes forgot to lock her door at all, was foolhardy.

Mady used her two keys and went in. The apartment, in the middle of the day, was tidy and silent and strange. The blinds were drawn, and the clock on the kitchen cabinet ticked rapidly to itself. Mady always had the feeling that it sounded cross, as if it were going *tut-tut-tut-tut-tut*, and would have shaken its head if it could.

The apartment was nice and cool.

Mady hurried, getting into her oldest shorts and shirt. Sue Ellen was waiting in the hall outside. Together they ran down to the street. They leaped shouting and laughing into the clear, sparkling, bubbling spray from the hydrant. Eyes closed, they shoved their faces into the fizz and froth of the water, getting their hair drenched, and their clothes.

It was marvelous. Mady stamped with pleasure. She decided it was like being in Niagara Falls.

"Niagara Falls! Niagara Falls!" she shouted above the din. "We're all in Niagara Falls!"

A boy doubled up, holding his knees to his chest, and rolled about. "I'm going over Niagara Falls in a barrel!" he yelled.

"Niagara Falls! Niagara Falls! Niagara, Niagara, Ni —Ni—agara—agara!" The children sang and shouted.

After a while the fireman came to turn the hydrant off. He stood with the wrench in his hand, watching the children and smiling. He looked as if he wanted to get into the rushing water with them.

But in a few minutes he said, "Sorry, kids, that's all for today," and turned off Niagara Falls with his wrench.

Sopping, soaking, dripping, Mady and Sue Ellen sloshed down the street back to their apartment building.

"For goodness' sake, go into the bathroom and change," said Mrs. Forrest. "You'll flood us out." But she sounded lively, as if the sight of them, smiling and dripping, made her happy.

Mady went across the hall, used her two keys again, and after she'd dried herself in the bathroom and got into her dress, took the towel and wiped up the floor. Her mother tried to keep things nice and was not as cheery and chirpy as Mrs. Forrest. Which was why

Mady usually played in Sue Ellen's apartment and not the other way around.

Mrs. Forrest had finished the ironing. She said that now she had to go marketing and do some other things and did the girls want to go with her.

"What are the other things?" asked Sue Ellen.

"Oh, you know. I'll visit a few people. It's summer. No need to hurry. I'll have some lemonade with Mrs. Gerez, most likely."

Sue Ellen and Mady decided they'd stay home.

"We'll have a lemonade party for our dolls," said Sue Ellen.

"That's a good idea," said her mother. "You'll find cookies in the cupboard, in case the dolls are hungry." She blew them a kiss.

"Bye, Momma."

"Bye, Aunt Lillian."

Mady had to go back across the hall and use her two keys all over again. She got her Chinese doll, Kim, her dancing doll, Vera, and her just doll doll, whose name was Sally. Sue Ellen had said she could only invite three, as that was all the room there was. She had only three dolls anyway, and that was all Sue Ellen had. Mrs. Guthrie said that was a lot, and that some little girls didn't have any. But Mady didn't know any girls without a doll.

Sue Ellen had a little round table and six little chairs and a plastic tea set for six. Her father had given them to her for Christmas, and here it was the beginning of July and nothing was broken.

Sue Ellen took better care of her things than Mady did, although Mrs. Forrest never said, "Be careful," and Mady's mother said it all the time.

Well, it was funny, thought Mady, looking at her dancing doll who had lost one leg, and at Sally who looked a sight but was her love. Her Chinese doll was practically perfect but also practically new, since Mady's birthday came at the end of June.

Well, there it was. Some people took better care than other people did. But it was summer, and no time to worry.

Sue Ellen had a baby doll, a boy doll, and a rag doll. The boy doll, Daniel, and the baby doll, who was just called Baby, were as good as new, but the rag doll had burst a seam. Sue Ellen sewed her up carefully, taking a long time, and the party couldn't begin until she was finished.

"I'm going to be a doctor when I grow up," said Sue Ellen, taking tiny stitches. "The kind that sews on people."

"You can't be a doctor," said Mady. "Doctors are men." She stood at the window, looking down at the boys who'd returned to their shooting, except for some who were playing stickball.

"Don't be silly," said Sue Ellen, biting off the thread. "There are lots of lady doctors and lady lawyers and lady policemen and lady taxi drivers and—"

"Lady astronauts," said Mady.

"Only they're Russian. We don't have one. Yet."

"And lady presidents."

"Well, I guess not yet, either," said Sue Ellen. She patted her rag doll. "There you are, Geneva. You're well enough to go to the party. Just don't over-do."

When all the dolls were seated, waiting, Mady and Sue Ellen went to the kitchen. They made a pitcher of pink lemonade, a big one, and then poured some of it into the tiny teapot that went with the plastic tea set. They put some cookies on a plate and broke up some very small pieces to put in front of each doll on a tiny plastic plate.

"Now," said Mady and Sue Ellen together, sitting on the floor. "Now, let's have the party."

Sue Ellen poured lemonade from the little teapot into the tiny teacups. She gave each doll a bit of cookie.

They had to talk for their dolls, and the Chinese doll, being the newest, got to speak first.

"Ting, ling, kow foo chop suey," said Kim, the Chinese doll, in Mady's voice but high and singing. "Kow ling chow mein foo!"

"What language you using, man?" said the rag doll in Sue Ellen's voice. "I come from Brooklyn and don't dig you a bit."

"Don't be silly," said Sally, the doll doll, in Mady's voice but deeper now. "He's speaking Chinese."

"Why?" asked Geneva.

"Oh, you are silly. Because he's Chinese, that's why. He comes from Hong Kong. It says so on his shoes," said Mady.

"Well, he isn't in Hong Kong now," said Sue Ellen. "So why doesn't he talk American?"

They had forgotten to use their doll voices, and for a moment they glared at each other, and the tea party was threatened.

Then Sue Ellen shrugged, moved Daniel slightly, and said in her boy-doll voice, "Man, that's the most. A visitor from Hong Kong." When neither Mady nor any of her dolls responded, Sue Ellen had Geneva stand up. "Let's have some of that lemonade," said Geneva. "And these dear little pieces of cookie. I'm hungry."

Mady and Sue Ellen poured their own lemonade and ate their own cookies, and then helped the dolls with theirs. The tea party was saved.

When they'd finished eating, Vera, the dancing doll, said, "I believe now I'll dance." Mady helped her up from the chair. "I will spin on my one leg like a ballerina," said Vera. Mady helped her to spin around the room, while Sue Ellen sang a song her father taught her.

> *Frère Jacques, Frère Jacques,*
> *Dormez-vous? Dormez-vous?*
> *Sonnez les matines, sonnez les matines,*
> *Ding dang dong. Ding dang dong.*

Vera danced for quite a while until Sue Ellen stopped singing and Geneva said, "Can't anybody else do anything?"

"What can you do?" asked Sally, the doll doll.

"I can sing," said Geneva, and sang just the way Sue Ellen had been singing. In fact, she sang the same song.

"Well, I've had enough of this," said Sally. "I want to do something too."

"Dada dada dada," said the baby doll.

"Let's go on a freedom march," said Daniel.

All the dolls got up, gathered into their owners' arms, and they stamped around the living room on their owners' feet, singing.

> *We shall overcome, we shall overcome,*
> *We shall overcome some day!*

"Martin Luther King is up there," said Daniel.

"Where? Where?" asked Vera, leaping high in the air.

"He's out of sight at the head of the parade. We're following him," said Daniel.

"Freedom now! Freedom now!" shouted all the dolls, even the Chinese doll and the baby doll.

They used Mady's and Sue Ellen's voices and Mady's and Sue Ellen's legs, and they stamped and shouted all around the room.

Suddenly, from underneath, there was a banging noise.

The dolls stopped marching. So did Sue Ellen and Mady. The banging noise came from the woman who lived downstairs. She was poking the ceiling with her broom, telling them to keep quiet and if they didn't they'd be sorry.

Sue Ellen and Mady knew the whole message, just from how the broom banged. They decided to keep quiet.

The dolls went back to the table, and their hostesses sat on the floor beside them. They finished up the lemonade and the last cookie.

"Would you go on a freedom march?" Mady asked Sue Ellen. "A real one?"

"How could I go on a freedom march? I'm too young."

"There are some kids go. Or they sit-in or pray-in. You know. Some of them even get in jail."

Mady's own father had been in jail in Mississippi. He had gone down to that state to get Negroes to register for voting and he hadn't ever come back, because one night he'd been shot, and he died. Mady didn't say anything about this now to Sue Ellen, but she thought that Sue Ellen could have mentioned something about it, just to show that she remembered Mady had had a father too, once upon a time.

But all Sue Ellen said was, "Well, I'm too young," in a stubborn voice.

"Well, but if you *weren't*, would you?" Mady persisted.

Sue Ellen narrowed her eyes, thinking. She'd seen on television what the freedom marches and the protests and the boycotts and the voter registration drives were like. Colored people being beat up and yelled at. Dogs biting them. Policemen hitting them on the head with clubs. She'd seen little kids with whole bunches of white grown-ups screaming at them because they wanted to go to school someplace. Or their parents wanted them to. Or the government did. It was awful, all those grown-up people hollering at those little kids.

Momma, when she saw it, said it was awful too. "But terrible things do happen in life, Sue Ellen," she'd said. "And they don't always happen to other people. And they don't always happen down South, either."

But Sue Ellen didn't want to think about it. She wanted to be safe and warm with Pop and Momma, with Mady and Mrs. Guthrie, with her friends from school and the teachers she had there that were nice, which all of them weren't, but some were.

Poor Mady's own father had got himself killed in a voter registration drive, but Sue Ellen didn't ever mention that to her because it might make her sad. Sue Ellen did not like people to be sad.

"I don't want to think about it," she said now to Mady. "Anyway, when we grow up," she added confidently, "it will all be over. There won't be any freedom marches or sit-ins or like that. Martin Luther King will fix it."

Mady sighed. Sue Ellen was her very best friend, but there was one thing you couldn't ever do with her and that was talk about anything serious. Especially not anything serious and sad too. Mady thought that being a Negro was both sad and serious lots of the time, but Sue Ellen just wouldn't talk about it.

"Well, it was a nice tea party," said Mady, "but I think the dolls are tired out now. They ought to go to bed."

"Yes, especially the baby doll," said Sue Ellen.

"She's got that grouchy look she gets when she's over-tired."

So Mady went back across the hall, using her keys for the fourth time, and gently put her dolls to bed on the windowsill all in a row on a blanket. Usually she just tossed them into a chair or even on the floor, until her mother told her to pick them up. But she had decided to be a better mother to her dolls from now on.

She felt sorry about Vera's lost leg and about Sally's battered appearance. The doll doll looked as if she had a permanent case of chicken pox, or had been left out on the fire escape in the rain, which, as it happened, was what *had* happened.

But what was past was past, as her mother often said. The thing was to do better from now on. Having decided this, she immediately felt better. Mady always felt better when she'd decided something, even if she hardly ever did what she'd decided.

Mostly, she realized, she did what Sue Ellen decided.

Summers were best of all. In any case Sue Ellen and Mady thought they were. It wasn't being out of school that pleased them best. For two years now they'd been going to school in a brand new building. The principal, Mr. Carmondy, was a man everybody liked, and so far Sue Ellen and Mady had been in the same class together and had had teachers they liked.

Lots of the kids around here absolutely hated school and were just waiting to get old enough to be drop-outs. But Sue Ellen and Mady liked school and didn't intend to be dropouts ever.

Still, being free—the way you were in summertime, just completely free to do anything you wanted, or not to do it—was marvelous. And Mady, who hated the cold, loved the way she could dash in and out of the apartment in the summertime. No jackets or boots or ice-crusted mittens. No freezing fingers when the mittens got lost.

In July, when people went around complaining about the heat and humidity, Mady just smiled and wished it would go on forever.

Sue Ellen's father, Mr. Forrest, who had gone to college for a couple of years and knew, Mady figured, just about more than anyone else did, even people who'd *finished* college, had said that Mady was a salamander.

"What's that?" Sue Ellen had asked jealously.

"Sort of a lizard. The Greeks believed it could live in the heart of the fire and not burn up."

Mady had wondered if she really liked being compared to a lizard, but Mr. Forrest, seeing her expression, had laughed. "It's a beautiful little slender creature, silky and swift," he'd told her.

Winters around here sometimes the furnaces went off and the apartments got cold, icy cold as the out-of-doors. That, to Mady, was horrible. The hottest of sultry days and nights were better. Oh, she loved the summertime, and Sue Ellen did too.

The trouble was that being free to do anything you wanted, or not do it, left you after a few weeks not sure sometimes what it was you wanted to do, or not do.

"What'll we do now?" Mady asked Sue Ellen when she'd put her dolls away on the windowsill and had returned to Sue Ellen's apartment.

Sue Ellen looked at the clock. Still pretty early. Her mother wouldn't be home probably for ages yet. Her father was due back at four o'clock, but that was a couple of hours off.

"Let's go walk around the ten-cent store."

"Did your momma say it's all right to?" Mady asked.

"She says if we stay together, like always. Did your momma?"

"She says do what Aunt Lillian says, as long as I'm with you, only be careful."

"Well, we're careful," Sue Ellen said impatiently.

"I mean, my gosh, do you want a policeman to go with us?"

"I wouldn't mind," said Mady, and Sue Ellen laughed. "We don't have any money," Mady added.

"We never have any money. Hardly ever. They don't charge for walking around."

The ten-cent store was seven blocks away, and by the end of their walk they were glad to get inside. It was air-conditioned. Mady liked air-conditioning because like the spray from the hydrant it was a sign of summer. Besides, you knew that when you went back on the street it would be hot again.

The two girls thought that a ten-cent store was about the best place in the world. Except maybe that outdoor swimming pool where the whole class had been taken just before school let out. They had gone on a subway and neither of them had any idea now of where it was.

But it had been neat, all right. They'd worn rented gray bathing suits, had hot dogs and Coke, and splashed around in this huge pool practically the whole day. Sue Ellen and Mady had to stay in the shallow part because neither of them could swim. But they'd pretended to, going along in the low water, heads up, hands on the bottom, kicking their legs. It had almost felt like swimming, but Mady had had to admit, looking at Sue Ellen humping along, that it didn't really look like swimming.

There had been a slide at the deep end, steep and shining, with water rushing down it. They'd looked at that longingly. Kids were absolutely flying from the top into the pool. Kids that knew how to swim.

Well, they didn't know where that swimming pool was and expected they wouldn't get to go again until next year.

"Can you think as far ahead as next year?" Mady asked now.

Sue Ellen considered. "I guess not. But I can think farther. I can think about being grown up."

"Anybody can do that. It's next year that's hard."

They often talked about what they were going to do when they grew up. Mady was going to be like people on television who worked at the zoo and took care of baby animals. Sue Ellen changed her mind all the time. Today she was going to be a doctor. Last week it had been an actress. Sometimes she said she was going to be a teacher and other times an airline hostess. You couldn't tell with Sue Ellen.

They were looking at beautiful colored glass beads and earrings, keeping their hands behind their backs so no one would think they were going to touch.

Ten-cent stores, Mrs. Forrest had told them one

day, had spies and cameras all over the place, watching dishonest people.

"We aren't dishonest," Sue Ellen had said. "So they won't be watching us."

"They watch everybody, just in case," Mrs. Forrest had said.

It had made Sue Ellen so angry that for a week she would not go to the ten-cent store at all. But now here she was, looking at the glass beads and earrings, keeping her hands behind her back.

"Where do you suppose the spies and cameras are?" she asked Mady.

They looked around. Nobody looked the least bit spyish, and of course they knew that these days cameras came so small that no one could ever spot them or guess the strange ways they were disguised. They could be in nailheads in the wall, or on the edges of somebody's spectacles. Anywhere.

"Well, I don't like it," Sue Ellen insisted. "*Watching* people. It's awful."

"So do I think so," said Mady. She meant it. Many times when she agreed with Sue Ellen it was because she wanted to be friendly, or didn't disagree, or didn't know whether she did or did not.

"It would be nice to buy something," she said, moving along the counter.

"What would you buy?"

"A goldfish," Mady said promptly. "And a bowl and some colored pebbles and a little castle with a door in it for my fish to swim in and out of."

They went and looked at the goldfish. They were in a great tank of clear water with a column of bubbles rising at one side and a lovely underwater forest arranged for the fish's pleasure. China mermaids and bridges were dotted here and there in the sandy bottom, and a skin diver floated among the fish who wandered through wands of water plants, opening and closing their mouths as if they were saying *ooh, ooh, oooh*.

Some were orange-gold, some yellow-gold, some gold spotted with freckles, and some weren't gold at all. There were a few beautiful black ones with tails like chiffon fans. That's the sort I'd have, thought Mady. A black goldfish.

There were also little green turtles, pushing the water away with tiny clawed feet. They skimmed along the bottom of the tank, then shot almost straight upward to poke their noses—like pencil dots—out of the water for a moment, and then down they went again.

There were snails, moving ever so slowly up the glass sides. They had shining spiral shells and little heads with horns. As the two girls watched, a snail who'd been clinging to a branch of the water plant suddenly let go and drifted down to land in a flurry in the sand.

"I just do love them," said Mady.

"Snails?" asked Sue Ellen, wrinkling her nose.

"Well, I don't exactly love *them*. Except they're all right. No, but the goldfish are gorgeous, aren't they? Especially those black ones with the fan tails."

"Oh, you like all animals," said Sue Ellen.

"So do you," Mady retorted.

"Not the way you do. I mean, I'm not just nuts and crazy over them."

But Mady loved all animals. Cats, dogs, the little gray city sparrows that ate crumbs from her windowsill. What she wanted to see on television was anything that had animals in it. The people programs didn't interest her. Sue Ellen, on the other hand, liked Westerns and those terrible ones where you tried to answer questions and win things for answering. Often Sue Ellen could answer the questions better than some of those grown-ups on the program, and she said that one day she was going to go on a program herself. Mady would've died first.

They wandered on.

"What would you buy?" Mady said.

"Huh? Oh, you mean if I could. Well, I guess I'd get my mother one of these aprons, with roses printed on it. Or maybe a dish towel with a map of London, like that one."

Mady wished that she'd said she'd buy her mother something. But she knew that if the time ever came, she'd still get the goldfish and the bowl and the colored pebbles and the little castle.

"Momma would probably like to have a goldfish to look at," she said defensively.

"Sure she would," said Sue Ellen. "Anybody would like a goldfish."

Mady felt somewhat better.

They inspected the pots and pans, passed up tools and nails, stopped in front of the toy counter. They looked for a long time at the different things.

Model cars, and tops, and bags of balloons, and dolls and jeeps and tractors and holsters with guns in them, and marbles and jacks, and painting sets and clay sets, and airplane and warship models, and rockets, and cutout dolls with wardrobes, and—it was almost confusing to look.

"What would you buy if you could buy anything here?" said Sue Ellen.

"I'd still buy the goldfish."

"I *said* something *here*."

"I wouldn't buy anything here. I'd buy the goldfish."

"Oh, for goodness' sakes," said Sue Ellen, sounding annoyed.

"What would you?"

Sue Ellen sighed, surveying the entire toy counter. "I guess I'd still buy the apron for my mother."

They laughed at that and went on to inspect the cosmetics, the paper supplies, the ribbon department, the glassware, the candy counter.

Some of the candy looked meltingly good.

"Oh, boy," said Sue Ellen. "Look at the nut rolls."

Mady said, "You know, it's funny, but your mouth really does water when you see something good to eat, doesn't it? I mean, it's not just something people say in books."

Suddenly, in spite of the tea party, they were too hungry to remain looking at candy and cookies, smelling the spicy aroma of hot dogs cooking on a grill, hearing the swish from spigots as ice cream sodas were created.

They left.

Outside, after the coldness of the store, the heat seemed to swarm at them. Sidewalks glittered with bits of mica, and they could smell hot tar where men had been repairing the street. Several blocks away the elevated train rumbled by, and that sounded hot too, and heavy.

"My goodness," said Sue Ellen. "We'll be cooked before we get home."

Even Mady found it pretty hot, but wouldn't give in and say so.

"Hey girls! Going my way?"

A taxi pulled up to the curb, and there was Sue Ellen's father.

"Hop in," he invited. "I'm on my way to the garage and can just fit in one more fare on my way."

"We can't pay you, driver," said Sue Ellen, climbing into the back seat of the cab. Mady scrambled in after her, feeling pretty sure that everyone was watching them, thinking how lucky they were.

"I'll settle for two smiles and a report on the day's activities," said Mr. Forrest. "What have you two done with yourselves today?"

"Nothing," they said together. And then, "Lots of things."

"We went to Niagara Falls," said Mady.

"And gave a tea party. Elegant, of course," said Sue Ellen.

"Six guests. And dancing."

"We went on a freedom march."

"With Martin Luther King."

"We went shopping for goldfish and aprons and a few other things."

"I don't see any packages," said Mr. Forrest, turning around for a second.

"Practice shopping," Mady explained.

"I see. Pretty good kind at that, I guess," said their chauffeur.

"Not all the time," Sue Ellen said darkly, but then she and her father laughed.

Mady leaned back, blinking. She loved Mr. Forrest. She wished—and when she'd been small, she'd even prayed—that he could be her own father. Now that she was older, she knew what a bad prayer it had been. Sue Ellen was her friend, and you don't pray a friend's father away from her.

Suddenly, terribly, Mady was missing her own father. Not just thinking about him as she had earlier that day, but missing him with this terrible pinching pain. Her *father* . . .

She was glad that Sue Ellen and Mr. Forrest were going on talking. If she had a little while to be quiet, to sort of close in on herself, she could keep from crying. She steadied herself against the back of the cab and took deep breaths and tried to listen to what they said.

"What kind of a day did you have, Pop?" Sue Ellen was asking.

"Remarkable. Truly remarkable," said Mr. Forrest.

He stopped for a light, turned, and looked at his passengers.

"I saved a man's life."

"Pop! What do you mean?" Sue Ellen gasped.

Mr. Forrest turned back to the traffic, drove on. "I didn't run over a guy," he said.

Sue Ellen burst out laughing. "Oh, *Pop*," she said reproachfully.

"I'm serious."

Sue Ellen was still giggling. "You haven't run over plenty of people just since we got in here. Did you save all their lives?"

"Some respect, young woman, please. I'll have you know that this cat jumped right in front of my hack. I practically threw the brakes on the street, stopping in time, and slewed almost into the fence over there on Park Avenue."

"It was a cat?" Mady said, sitting up.

"No, no," said Mr. Forrest. "I meant a man. You know. Anyway, he almost demolished me so I could keep from demolishing him, if you see what I mean. So, I saved his life. He thought so, and I thought so. So it must've been a fact."

"What did you do? I mean *then*. Afterward," Sue Ellen asked breathlessly.

Mr. Forrest shrugged his heavy shoulders. "Drove him home. He lives in this big duplex on Park."

"Why did he walk in front of your cab?"

"Who knows? Thinking about something else, he said, and didn't watch the lights."

"He sounds sort of dumb."

"Oh, no. A nice guy. Well-spoken. Careless, you could say."

"My goodness, Pop," said Sue Ellen, wriggling happily. "You're a hero!" How impressed everyone was going to be! She could scarcely wait to get home. As the cab turned into their own street, she leaned forward, hand on the door handle, ready to escape and begin spreading the news.

"Now, look here," said Mr. Forrest, who could, both girls felt, read their minds. "Look here, Sue Ellen, Mady. I suppose I shouldn't have said anything about this at all, but it had just happened and I *felt* like talking about it. But"—he fixed them, each in turn, with his brown, deep-seeing eyes—"I rely on you not to say anything to your friends. To anybody."

"Ah, gee, Pop."

"Not a word. If you'll think it over a bit, you'll see that you'd just be making a fool of me. Save a guy's life by not running over him, indeed."

"But you said—"

"Never mind what I said. Listen to what I'm saying."

"Okay," Sue Ellen said reluctantly.

"That's better. Now, run along."

"You mean we can't even tell Momma?"

Mr. Forrest rubbed the back of his neck, pushing his cap forward. "Me and my big mouth," he said. "I'll tell your mother. By this time it all sounds sort of ridiculous, doesn't it?"

"Not to me it doesn't—" Sue Ellen began, and was interrupted again.

"It does to me," said Mr. Forrest firmly. "So forget it, see?"

"Okay, Pop," Sue Ellen said again.

"Yes, Uncle Dan," said Mady, when he looked at her.

Mr. Forrest wasn't her uncle, not really. But she'd called him that for years. She called Mrs. Forrest Aunt Lillian. Her own real aunts and uncles lived in Alabama, and she hadn't seen them except so long ago that she'd forgotten. She had cousins too, down there. But here the Forrests were all the family she and her mother had.

Within herself Mady knew that she wouldn't trade the Forrests for a thousand real cousins and aunts and uncles. But she never said so to her mother, who wrote to the family in Alabama once in a while, and once in a while talked about Uncle Jack or Aunt Pam or Cousin Hank.

Mady had once asked her mother why they didn't go to visit these relatives, or why the relatives didn't come up here to visit. Momma had said the Alabama kin was too poor to come traipsing to New York City, and that she wouldn't go down there herself for a solid gold tiara.

"What's a tiara?" Mady had asked, forgetting about the relatives.

When they got out of the cab, Mr. Forrest said, "Tell your mother I'll be home as soon as I garage the hack. Won't be long. And you two stick around. I've got a surprise for you."

He drove off with a flip of his hand, and the two girls stood staring after him with love and pleasure. A surprise!

"What do you suppose . . . now, just what can it be?" Sue Ellen wondered.

Mady couldn't answer, she felt so happy. A surprise.

They sat on the stoop to wait, watching the boys, who had given up killing for stickball. They made as much noise, and fought more, playing games as they did when they were shooting. But anyway, they were occupied. If they hadn't been, Sue Ellen and Mady would have gone upstairs.

Boys, they had found, couldn't be idle without getting restless. When they got restless, they teased, and when they teased, after a while they tended to turn mean.

"They're funny, aren't they?" Mady said, watching them as they swung, hit, missed, ran, yelled, and shouted in triumph or disagreement.

"How do you mean?"

"Well, like you practically never see just one boy. Or even two boys, very much. They come in such bunches."

Mr. Forrest said the neighborhood they lived in was a racial stew. "Something of everything," he said. "White, colored, Oriental. Name it, we've got it."

But colored, Oriental, or white, in any mixture, to Mady's way of thinking, boys came in bunches.

"That's what makes them scary, I suppose," Sue Ellen said. She was not as fearful of them as Mady was, but Sue Ellen was not timid by nature. Still, she knew what Mady meant.

Girls, if they had nothing to do, could usually think of something to do, like a doll's tea party or a pretend shopping trip. Even, if they were restless or angry or unhappy, going someplace to cry. If boys were restless or angry or unhappy, they didn't go off by themselves. They got together and looked for someone to take it out on.

The best thing girls could do was stay out of their way.

Mrs. Forrest—when Sue Ellen had said something about the boys and how she and Mady wished they would all go away and live somewhere else, like maybe the North Pole, because then the neighborhood would be nice and peaceful—had shaken her head.

"No, no, *no*," she had said. "You mustn't talk like that. You must try to understand people, Sue Ellen. Not wish them out of your life, as if they had no right to exist. The boys around here, they're angry lots of the time—the way poor people get angry when they see all the things they can't have or do, when they think of all the things they can never be, just because they are poor. It's like a sore that won't heal. Like a huge unfairness that you can't do anything about. That's why they get so wild, sometimes. So destructive."

"Well, we're poor," Sue Ellen had said, not convinced. "And we don't get wild and destructive."

"We are not poor. We have a decent place to live and good food. We have love. Love's a kind of richness lots of those kids in the street never have. When you're without love and when you see all there is in the world that will never be for you, you get so you want to smash something, to show that you're *there*. To prove that you count."

"Why does smashing things or scaring people make anybody know you're there?"

Mrs. Forrest had shaken her head. "I don't know the *whys* of these things, lovey. I only know the *ares*. And smashing seems to work, somehow. At least somebody pays attention to you."

"Yeah, the cops."

"Maybe better than no attention at all," Mrs. Forrest had said, sounding tired.

Just the same, Mady and Sue Ellen were never allowed out at night. And at night even Mrs. Forrest locked her door.

It was all very hard to figure out. Lots of times their parents or the teachers said to them, "You'll understand when you're older." Mady and Sue Ellen figured it would have to wait until then, because right now they didn't understand any of it—the fear in the streets; the bolted doors; the roving gangs of older boys and girls, demanding attention from the police if from no one else.

Still, they weren't afraid in the daytime. Not if they were together and knew Mr. Forrest was going to come home soon.

"Hey, there he is!" said Sue Ellen, jumping up.

Mr. Forrest came strolling down the block, in his shirt-sleeves, carrying his jacket over one arm and a package under the other. He grinned as Mady and Sue Ellen came dashing to meet him.

"Well, well," he said. "To what do I owe the pleasure of this salutation?"

"Just glad to see you, Pop."

Mady tried not to stare at the package, but her eyes kept going back to it.

"Is that the surprise?" Sue Ellen blurted.

"Mmm . . . might be. Now that you draw my attention to the matter, it is. Should have known all this ceremony wasn't for my beaux yeux."

"What's your bowz-yuh, Uncle Dan?" said Mady, impressed almost beyond bearing. It was French he was talking, she knew that much.

"My fine eyes," he explained, as they started upstairs. "My good looks, as it were."

"Well, it was for those," Mady said, but in such a whisper that neither Uncle Dan nor Sue Ellen, squabbling amiably over who was to carry the package, heard her.

Mrs. Forrest was getting dinner. She turned when they came in and said, "Did you remember that your mother is switching to the three to eleven shift today, Mady? You're to eat with us."

"Oh, no. I'd forgotten." Mady was ashamed of herself for feeling a rush of pleasure at these unexpected hours with the Forrests.

Mady loved her mother dearly, and she liked her too. What she couldn't do, lots of the time, was get along with her. Mrs. Guthrie worked very hard at the hospital and had, besides, to keep house and market and cook for Mady and herself. Mady tried to help sometimes, but the fact was—and she and her mother both knew it—she was more of a hindrance than a help. She was a slow-moving person, not like a salamander that way at all. Her mother was lively and quick as a squirrel. "Oh, darling, get *out* of the way," she'd say. "I can do this and six other things besides while you're making up your mind."

It was true, it was true. Many many times Mady had made up her mind to think fast, to act quickly, to do things *one, two, three, zip zap in a hurry.* It usually came out to something getting broken.

"Mady O'Grady's a dreamy lady . . ."

She heard it distantly, blinked, shook her head, and smiled at Uncle Dan.

"Mady O'Grady's *the* dreamiest lady," he chanted.

"Pop, what's the surprise?" Sue Ellen said, flicking an irritable glance in Mady's direction.

Mady pretended not to see. "Yes, what *is* it?" she said, trying to sound eager too, although Sue Ellen's expression had chilled her interest. "What is is *is* it?"

she shrilled, and gave a little jump to emphasize her anticipation, because she didn't want to disappoint Uncle Dan.

"Oh, for Pete's sake," Sue Ellen said. "Do you have to be so dopey?"

Overwhelmed, Mady rushed from the apartment. With tears burning her face, blinking her eyes, she tried to push a key into the wrong lock. She fumbled, sniffled, her head tipped slightly backward, waiting for the footsteps, the approach she knew would come.

It was Aunt Lillian who walked across the hall, saying, "Mady—lovey—don't be upset. Sue Ellen's sorry she was cross. Come back, do."

Mady ran her hand across her nose and mouth, took a deep breath, and another. She couldn't talk yet.

"Here's some tissue," said Mrs. Forrest. "Blow your nose, and come to dinner. We're having meat loaf, your favorite."

"All right, Aunt Lillian. I'm sorry, I'm sorry I was dopey. Sometimes it—I don't know—"

"It takes you by surprise. Well, dopiness does that to all of us. And don't think all of us aren't dopes at one time or another."

"But with me it *shows* so," Mady wailed. She was, indeed, willing to believe that other people were as dumb and silly as she was sometimes, but never seemed to notice anyone but herself.

When she pointed this out, Mrs. Forrest said it was probably because she didn't notice much about other people at all. "It's the way people are at your age," she said comfortingly, as if it were the right way for Mady to be. "You'll outgrow it."

"You're sure?"

"Perfectly sure."

Mr. Forrest and Sue Ellen were sitting on the sofa, the package still unopened between them.

"Come on," said Sue Ellen, patting the seat beside her. "We're *waiting*."

Still sniffling a little, Mady smiled and went to stand in front of them.

"Here," said Sue Ellen, handing her the package. "Here, you open it."

It was a kite. A kite so beautiful that when Mr. Forrest had it assembled they all stood around, transfixed. Blue and red, with a wingspread of almost eighteen inches and a snaky white tail. It seemed to glow in the room.

"Like a bird out of a jungle," Mady breathed. "It's beautiful, Uncle Dan. Just heavenly beautiful."

"Shall we give it its first flying lesson? There's a good wind up, not too gusty." He looked at his wife. "Time before dinner?" he asked.

She laughed. "Could I say No?"

They filed out of the apartment after him, up the

stairs to the roof, collecting a few neighbors on the way.

"These city buildings and the heat that's generated from them," Mr. Forrest explained, "make perfect air currents, like those in canyons out west. Perfect for the art of kite flying. You all understand, I trust, that it is an art. Takes skill, insight, hindsight, foresight, a delicate hand, a far-seeing eye, patience, judgment—" He broke off, frowning. "What happened to the wind?"

Sue Ellen stuck a finger in her mouth, held it up high. A slight coolness touched it on the fingernail side. "There's a wind, Pop. Put up your finger and see."

"When I came home the wind was making eddies of litter up and down the street. Practically a trash tornado. Now, just where did that wind go?" he demanded, looking at them sternly.

Sue Ellen and Mady giggled, as glances were exchanged all around. Some people couldn't tell with Mr. Forrest just when he was fooling. But they always could.

"Ah-hah! There it is!"

Everyone sprang to attention.

"Now," said Mr. Forrest, "observe that I stand with my back to this wind, the velocity of which I judge to be between ten and twelve miles an hour, with minor gusts. Releasing just a little of string, I wait until—ah, there we are, *there* we are—"

The kite fluttered, sprang up and down in Mr. Forrest's hand, tugged away from him, flew upward slightly, dipped down, started up again, as the watchers and the flyer held their breath and with the very stance of their bodies tried to give buoyancy to the white-tailed red and blue bird.

One hand holding the stick around which the string was wound, the other holding the string itself—releasing it gently, a little at a time—Mr. Forrest talked—explaining, cajoling, praising the kite when it seemed about to take wing, reassuring it when it dived roofward again, all the time miraculously keeping it aloft.

A little more and a little more until at last, gloriously, the wind swooped beneath their kite and bore it skyward. When it was well up, sailing freely at the end of its long string, Mr. Forrest, just by turning his wrist, sent it into beautiful sweeps and dives, drawing it down a little then giving it its head so that it flew upward and away to hover far above them.

They stood with their heads thrown back, watching until their necks ached, then watching still. It was turning dark when at last, with an air of peaceful satisfaction, Mr. Forrest began to wind the string, to bring the kite home again out of the sky.

A TRAINFUL OF STRANGERS

by Eleanor Hull

Saturday morning: ten-year-old Susan and her brother Hal, who was twelve, were on their way to downtown New York, because they had gotten tickets from their school to see the TV show, Science Searchlight.

The bus turned onto the Thruway. The towers of the city loomed beyond the park, floating on morning mist (or smog), and looking farther off and taller than they really were, than any real towers could be.

"I can't believe it!" Susan said, her feelings boiling

over again. "Just us, going to New York by ourselves! What an adventure!"

"It's not an adventure," said Hal. "It's real. It's Science. I don't see what you're going for; girls aren't interested in Science."

"They are too!" said Susan indignantly. She thought about it. She wasn't, really. But she could be if she wanted to. It was just that there were so many more interesting things to be interested in.

Anyway, Science Searchlight wasn't just Science, it was a TV Show. Susan had never seen a TV Show in person.

The bus pulled up at the subway station and honked madly at a shiny black car that had stopped to drop somebody off. It dropped a boy off.

"Oh, look, there's John Kent Haven!" said Susan.

"Being hand-delivered by his Mommy," agreed Hal.

The long train, jointed like a caterpillar, waited at the top of the long iron staircase. It panted gently, with all its doors wide open, as if it couldn't wait to snap its jaws shut on the people and roar away with them. Susan dashed into the first car to make sure of not being left, only to see Hal walking on outside the cars. What the—? Well—Susan ducked out again and raced after him.

"Why—?"

"Saves time to be up front," he informed her.

As they went forward there were fewer people, and the first car was occupied only by John Kent Haven.

Seeing him, Hal stopped short, but it was too late to turn back. "Hi," he said, passing up John Kent Haven and sitting across the aisle at the far end.

John Kent Haven grunted and looked out the window.

Susan had really hoped Tommy O'Donnell might decide to take one of the tickets and come, but no, out of their whole school here was nobody but skinny old stuck-up John Kent Haven. So it didn't really matter that Mother had made her comb down her hair. Unless she were to meet some Stranger.

A fat man waddled into the car and settled down with his newspaper, and then came a spidery woman wearing clean white gloves. A girl with long hair and glasses. A plump light Negro boy, very neatly dressed.

The train gasped and stopped breathing, as if it had given up hope all at once and died. Then its doors suddenly slid together and it moved matter-of-factly off along the iron trestle.

Why did they call it a *subway* out here, where it went way up in the air? People looked odd from the top; Susan watched them crawling along the sidewalks and into the shops. Then the train stopped at a crow's nest of a station, and some more people got on.

Further on they collected a little Spanish-looking girl who glanced timidly out of the corners of her eyes, and smoothed her skirt carefully beneath her, like an old lady, before she sat down across from Susan.

The train rumbled on between the dirty upstairs windows of old tenements, between haughty tall units of new housing developments. Then the street came up and the train went down and they were underground, with ghosts staring in at the windows—their own reflections, looking back at them. Susan's face, solemn and opalescent, hovered on the windowpane between the fat man, who was nothing but knees and a newspaper, and the thin woman, stiff as a plaster dress model except for her fingers in the white gloves that kept mechanically working at her black leather purse.

At 125th two Negro boys got on. They wore old dungarees, the kind Hal might wear to play ball in, but their jackets—Hal would never have worn either of those jackets, anywhere, any time. One had patches all over it—around the armholes, on the elbows, and down the front; and the other was a sleazy kind of artificial black leather.

Underprivileged, thought Susan.

She glanced at her brother, who was gazing at the newcomers over sternly crossed arms. Susan immediately felt sympathetic toward them, especially the short chubby button-nosed one with the patches, who was racing down the aisle.

"C'mon James, let's go up here," he was urging. "Where you sees the track jumping at you, like."

"Yeh, yeh, yeh," said his tall thin companion tolerantly, sauntering after. "Don't get in a sweat, Dobbs Henry, I'm follering."

Juvenile delinquents, thought Susan.

Heads turned all the way, eyes watchfully following the two young outsiders. They reached the front window and hunched to peer out.

There was a shrieking of iron wheels on iron tracks. The train stopped. The noise hushed so suddenly the world seemed to have stopped. The lights went out.

It seemed as if Susan's thoughts went out too, as the whole world vanished into silence and darkness.

The emergency lights went on, pale and sickly, and Susan found she could breathe again. She peered through the murk at the others, who were peering through the murk back.

"If this isn't the limit!" said the fat man across the aisle. "Third time this year I've got stuck in the subway!"

The train gave a lurch and a gasp, started up, shuddered violently, stopped again. The emergency lights went out, then on again.

The rear door of the car popped open and the conductor hurried in, swinging a flashlight. "Just a power failure," he said briskly. "We'll have it fixed in a jiffy." He opened the front door and jumped with a thud onto the tracks.

Two other thuds followed. Then a roar from the impatient conductor.

"You brats get back in there!" The boys scrambled back and the conductor's face appeared behind them, ferociously lighted from below by the flashlight.

"You could get electrocuted!" he warned, and disappeared again.

"Eeeee-lectrocuted!" echoed the boy called James, and there was a storm of hiccuppy giggles from his friend.

Some of the passengers crowded down to the front of the train to try to see what was happening.

"I can't see. What's going on?" asked John Kent Haven.

"They brung a bunch of guys in a handcar," reported the round-faced boy. "They got flashlights. Now they standing around talking things over."

"Prob'ly something got on the tracks. The other day up at Mt. Vernon (that's where I live, Mt. Vernon) somebody threw a baby buggy on the train tracks, and the trains couldn't run for two hours." (Whose voice was that? Oh, it must be that neat-looking Negro boy.)

"Baby buggy!" repeated the crackling voice of James Leather-Coat. "Listen at that, Dobbs Henry! Whose baby buggy, Kid? Yours?"

Hoodlums, thought Susan. *The trainload of trapped people were terrorized by two young gangsters.*

"Much less than a baby buggy could do it," went on the unperturbed voice. "Anything that breaks the connection."

"But, two hours!" protested the white-gloved lady. "Why, I'm on my way to see my sister in the hospital; I've got to get there before noon!"

The fat man came blundering back up the aisle, stepped heavily on Susan's foot, and sat down. "I daresay we all have things to do, of more or less importance," he said reprovingly.

"At least, we all think our own things are important," said someone with a laugh in her voice.

"Well, ours really are," said Hal. "We're due at the CBS-TV station at eleven o'clock."

"Really? How funny!" said the laughing voice. "So am I!"

"You mean you-all on TV?" exclaimed Dobbs Henry. "You sing or dance or something?"

"Sing or dance? *Me?*" said Hal.

"You're going to the Science Searchlight program, right?" said the Mt. Vernon boy. "You got tickets for it at school, right? That's me, too."

"If there are workmen out there, why don't they get the track fixed?" fumed the fat man. "What in the world is holding them up?"

"My poor sister will be wondering what could have happened to me," lamented the lady. "It isn't good for her health to worry."

"I sure did want to be at that broadcast," said the Mt. Vernon boy. "Now I wish I'd stayed home, I could at least have seen it. It's going to be about Quasars."

"Whatcha mean, Quasars?" (Dobbs Henry again.)

One of the young hoodlums showed a surprising interest in the rich children's affairs, thought Susan. (Rich? Well, richer than Dobbs Henry.)

"Radio waves," said Hal.

"No, they're not," said John Kent Haven vehemently. "They're quasi-stellar radio sources."

"Whoopee!" jeered the black-coated boy.

The other hoodlum worked off his aggressions by making nasty remarks about everybody, thought Susan.

"That's right, quasi-stellar radio sources," repeated the Mt. Vernon boy approvingly. "Gosh, how do you remember those big words?"

"What I like," said the laughing voice, though more seriously, "is the thought that we'll be able to see something that happened billions of years ago. Imagine! See it happening! Only of course, now we won't."

Susan jerked her head around. Hal never told her it would be anything like that. That would be worthwhile. But could she believe it? The speaker must be that girl with stringy black hair. She must be smart, though.

"If we're all going to the same place, we ought to get acquainted," said the boy from Mt. Vernon. "I'm Terry McIlvane."

"I'm Jennifer Morgenstern, from Yonkers," said the girl with dark hair.

A soft, breathless voice, not heard before, almost whispered, "I'm Cecilia Lopez. I go to that program too."

"We're Hal and Susan Hunter from White Plains, and over there's John Kent Haven. From our same school."

"Well, take a bow, Dobbs Henry, this gotta be our turn," said that intrusive voice from up front. It was maddening, like soap in your eyes. "Tell 'em we from Harlem. Sure 'nuff? Harlem?—Sure 'nuff."

"But we got no tickets to no show," said his friend. "Say, James, I bet them's the tickets Mr. Levy told us about. I thought at the time we shoulda took 'em."

"Yeh—they were free, weren't they?" said the other. "Nothin' for nothin'."

"If they can't fix this train," said the fat man, "they should get us out of here. We could go along the catwalk. Seems to me there's very little consideration—"

"Maybe we're blocked by another train," said the lady. "Maybe the exits are shut off. The conductor should come back and inform us, in any case."

"Maybe he'll never come back, Lady," said the one called James. "Maybe we'll never get out. Maybe we is all buried alive in here together! What a comedown!" He laughed.

Nobody else laughed.

That was the tragic day when the subway tunnels of New York finally gave way under the strain, thought Susan. *And whole trainloads of passengers were crushed by the weight of the great city.*

She thought of all the rocks and pavement and buildings. Was it really getting harder to breathe? Was her heart really pounding and her ears beginning to ring?

"Ay, *mi madre,* is it true? Buried alive?" The little Spanish girl had slipped across the aisle for company.

"No, of course not," said Susan in a tone that came out of her tight throat surprisingly calm and confident.

(Why, that was the tone Mother always used to make *her* feel better! Was that all there was to it—did Mother just *say* those things?)

The smoky darkness seemed to seep out of the tunnel and spread over the whole world . . .

And then a bright coin of light flew through the gloom and leaped into the car; the conductor's voice followed it, and lastly, the conductor himself bounded in, his cap pushed back and a grin on his face.

"All fixed up! Everybody O.K.?"

The lights went on. All the dim silhouettes that had been nothing but human beings in general turned suddenly into flesh and blood people with all sorts of peculiarities. Jennifer had braces on her teeth and thick glasses. The fat man, though so confident in the dark, immediately hid himself in his newspaper again, as though shy, in the light.

James and Dobbs Henry hunched at the front, muttering and snickering. It was hard to believe they had ever been part of the general conversation.

"We're too late for the show," said the boy from Mt. Vernon.

"I wonder if they'll give us tickets for next week,"

said Hal. "Maybe we could use the same ones." He absently fumbled in his pockets, then looked accusingly at Susan. "Where's your sweater?"

Susan looked around vaguely. Her sweater. When it got hot, she must have taken it off. But where?

"You left it in the bus," said Hal. "Stupid!"

Susan bit her lip. Cecilia could hear. Maybe Jennifer, too.

Jennifer didn't seem to have heard. She said, "Are you going to the broadcast next week?"

"If my teacher will fix it up again about meeting me at the station," said Terry. "So Mother will let me go."

"Same with us," said Hal. "Say, how's about we try to get together, and all go? Under the station clock at quarter to eleven?"

Nobody answered. Nobody could, because the train had let out a terrific bellow and started off. In the uproar they could no longer hear each other, and it was embarrassing to stare, so once again everyone was separate, and the eyes of all looked past each other.

Again, they were all strangers, thought Susan.

IT'S LIKE THIS, CAT

by Emily Neville

Fourteen-year-old Dave Mitchell persuaded his parents to let him keep the stray tiger tomcat who adopted him. New York apartments aren't especially convenient for cats, and Dave's father thought a dog would be educational; but Cat got the situation under control, and even a summer vacation trip with him was a success, as Dave tells it. The school year began well, too. . . .

Back home I'm pretty busy right away, on account of starting in a new school, Charles Evans Hughes High.

It's different from the junior high, where I knew half the kids, and also my whole homeroom there went from one classroom to another together. At Hughes everyone has to get his own schedule and find the right classroom in this immense building, which is about the size of Penn Station. There are about a million kids in it—actually about two thousand—most of whom I never saw before. Hardly any of the Stuyvesant Town and Peter Cooper Village kids come here because it isn't their district. However, walking back across Fifth Avenue one day, I see one kid I know from Peter Cooper. His name is Ben Alstein. I ask him how come he is at Hughes.

"My dad wanted me to get into Peter Stuyvesant High School—you know, the genius factory, city-wide competitive exam to get in. Of course I didn't make it. Biggest Failure of the Year, that's me."

"Heck, I never even tried for that. But how come you're here?"

"There's a special science course you can qualify for by taking a math test. Then you don't have to live in the district. My dad figures as long as I'm in something special, there's hope. I'm not really very interested in science, but that doesn't bother him."

So after that Ben and I walk back and forth to school together, and it turns out we have three classes together, too—biology and algebra and English. We're both relieved to have at least one familiar face to look for in the crowd. My old friend Nick, aside from not really being my best friend anymore, has gone to a Catholic high school somewhere uptown.

On the way home from school one Friday in September, I ask Ben what he's doing Monday and Tuesday, the Jewish holidays.

"Tuesday I got to get into my bar mitzvah suit and go to synagogue and over to Brooklyn to my grandmother's. Monday I don't have to do anything special. Come on over with your roller skates and we'll get in the hockey game."

"I skate on my tail," I say, because it's true, and it would be doubly true in a hockey game. I try quick to think up something else. We're walking down the block to my house, and there's Cat sitting out front, so I say, "Let's cruise around and get down to Fulton Fish Market and pick up some fish heads for my cat."

"You're a real nut, aren't you?" Ben says. He doesn't say it as if he minds—just mentioning the fact. He's an easygoing kind of guy, and I think most of the time he likes to let someone else make the plans. So he shrugs and says, "O.K."

I introduce him to Cat. Ben looks him in the eye, and Cat looks away and licks his back. Ben says, "So I got to get you fresh fish for Rosh Hashanah, huh?"

Cat jumps down and rubs from back to front against Ben's right leg and from front to back against his left leg and goes to lie down in the middle of the sidewalk.

"See? He likes you," I say. "He won't have anything to do with most guys, except Tom."

"Who's Tom?"

So I tell Ben all about Tom and the cellar and his father disappearing on him.

"Gee," says Ben, "I thought I had trouble with my father practically telling me how to breathe better every minute, but at least he doesn't disappear. What does Tom do now?"

"Works at the flower shop, right down there at the corner."

Ben feels around in his pockets a minute. "Hey, I got two bucks I was supposed to spend on a textbook. Come on and I'll buy Mom a plant for the holidays, and you can introduce me to Tom."

We go down to the flower shop, and at first Tom frowns because he thinks we've just come to kid around. Ben tells him he wants a plant, so then he makes a big thing out of showing him all the plants, from the ten-dollar ones on down, so Mr. Palumbo will see he's doing a good job. Ben finally settles on a funny-looking cactus that Tom says is going to bloom pretty soon.

Ben goes along home and I arrange to pick him up on Monday. I wait around outside until I see Tom go out on a delivery and ask him how he likes the job. He says he doesn't really know yet, but at least the guy is decent to work for, not like the filling-station man.

I sleep late Monday and go over to Peter Cooper about eleven. A lot of kids are out in the playgrounds, and some fathers are there tossing footballs with them and shouting "Happy New Year" to each other. It sounds odd to hear people saying that on a warm day in September.

Ben and I wander out of the project and he says, "How do we get to this Fulton Street?"

I see a bus that says "Avenue C" on it stopping on Twenty-third Street. Avenue C is way east, and so is Fulton Street, so I figure it'll probably work out. We get on. The bus rockets along under the East Side Drive for a few blocks and then heads down Avenue C, which is narrow and crowded. It's a Spanish and Puerto Rican neighborhood to begin with, then farther downtown it's mostly Jewish. Lots of people are out on the street shaking hands and clapping each other on the back, and the stores are all closed.

Every time the bus stops, the driver shouts to some of the people on the sidewalk, and he seems to know a good many of the passengers who get on. He asks

them about their jobs, or their babies, or their aunt
who's sick in Bellevue. This is pretty unusual in New
York, where bus drivers usually act like they hate
people in general and their passengers in particular.
Suddenly the bus turns off Avenue C and heads west.

Ben looks out the window and says, "Hey, this is
Houston Street. I been down here to a big delicatessen. But we're not heading downtown anymore."

"Probably it'll turn again," I say.

It doesn't, though, not till clear over at Sixth Avenue. By then everyone else has got off and the bus
driver turns around and says, "Where you two headed
for?"

It's funny, a bus driver asking you that, so I ask
him, "Where does this bus go?"

"It goes from Bellevue Hospital down to Hudson
Street, down by the Holland Tunnel."

"Holy crow!" says Ben. "We're liable to wind up in
New Jersey."

"Relax. I don't go that far. I just go back up to
Bellevue," says the driver.

"You think we'd be far from Fulton Fish Market?" I
say.

The driver gestures vaguely. "Just across the island."

So Ben and I decide we'll get off at the end of the

line and walk from there. The bus driver says, "Have a nice hike."

"I think there's something fishy about this," says Ben.

"That's what we're going to get, fish," I say, and we walk. We walk quite a ways.

Ben sees a little Italian restaurant down a couple of steps, and we stop to look at the menu in the window. The special for the day is lasagna, and Ben says, "Boy, that's for me!"

We go inside, while I finger the dollar in my pocket and do some fast mental arithmetic. Lasagna is a dollar, so that's out, but I see spaghetti and meat balls is seventy-five cents, so that will still leave me bus fare home.

A waiter rushes up, wearing a white napkin over his arm like a banner, and takes our order. He returns in a moment with a shiny clean white linen tablecloth and a basket of fresh Italian bread and rolls. On a third trip he brings enough chilled butter for a family and asks if we want coffee with lunch or later. Later, we say.

"Man, this is living!" says Ben as he moves in on the bread.

"He treats us just like people."

Pretty soon the waiter is back with our lasagna and

spaghetti, and he swirls around the table as if he were dancing. "Anything else now? Mind the hot plates, very hot! Have a good lunch now. I bring the coffee later."

He swirls away, the napkin over his arm making a little breeze, and circles another table. It's a small room, and there are only four tables eating, but he seems to enjoy acting like he was serving royalty at the Waldorf. When we're just finished eating, he comes back with a pot of steaming coffee and a pitcher of real cream.

I'm dolloping the cream in, and it floats, when a thought hits me: We got to leave a tip for this waiter.

I whisper to Ben, "Hey, how much money you got?"

He reaches in his pocket and fishes out a buck, a dime, and a quarter. We study them. Figure coffees for a dime each, and the total check out to be $1.95. We've got $2.35 between us. We can still squeak through with bus fare if we only leave the waiter a dime, which is pretty cheap.

At that moment he comes back and refills our coffee cups and asks what we will have for dessert.

"Uh, nothing, nothing at all," I say.

"Couldn't eat another thing," says Ben.

So the waiter brings the check and along with it a

plate of homemade cookies. He says, "My wife make. On the house."

We both thanked him, and I look at Ben and he looks at me. I put down my dollar and he puts down a dollar and a quarter.

"Thank you, gentlemen, thank you. Come again," says the waiter.

We walk into the street, and Ben spins the lone remaining dime in the sun. I say, "Heads or tails?"

"Huh? Heads."

It comes up heads, so Ben keeps his own dime. He says, "we could have hung onto enough for *one* bus fare, but that's no use."

"No use at all. 'Specially if it was yours."

"Are we still heading for Fulton Street?"

"Sure. We got to get fish for Cat."

"It better be for free."

We walk, threading across Manhattan and downtown. I guess it's thirty or forty blocks, but after a good lunch it doesn't seem too far.

You can smell the fish market when you're still quite a ways off. It runs for a half a dozen blocks alongside the East River, with long rows of sheds divided into stores for the different wholesalers. Around on the side streets there are bars and fish restaurants. It's too bad we don't have Cat with us because he'd love sniffing at all the fish heads and guts and stuff on the street. Fish market business is done mostly in the morning, I guess, and now men are hosing down the streets and sweeping fish garbage up into piles. I get a guy to give me a bag and select a couple of the choicer —and cleaner—looking bits. I get a nice red snapper head and a small whole fish, looks like a mackerel. Ben acts as if fish guts make him sick, and as soon as I've got a couple he starts saying "Come on, come on, let's go."

I realize when we're leaving that I don't even notice the fish smell anymore. You just get used to it. We walk uptown, quite a hike, along East Broadway and across Grand and Delancey. There's all kinds of intriguing smells wafting around here: hot breads and pickles and fish cooking. This is a real Jewish neighborhood, and you can sure tell it's a holiday from the smell of all the dinners cooking. And lots of people are out in their best clothes gabbing together. Some of the men wear black skullcaps, and some of them have big black felt hats and long white beards. We go past a crowd gathering outside a movie house.

"They're not going to the movies," Ben says. "On holidays sometimes they rent a movie theater for services. It must be getting near time. Come on, I got to hurry."

We trot along the next twenty blocks or so, up First Avenue and to Peter Cooper.

"So long," Ben says. "I'll come by Wednesday on the way to school."

He goes off spinning his dime, and too late I think to myself that we could have had a candy bar.

Ben and I both take biology, and the first weekend assignment we get, right after Rosh Hashanah, is to find and identify an animal native to New York City and look up its family and species and life cycle.

"What's a species?" says Ben.

"I don't know. What's a life cycle?"

We both scratch our heads, and he says, "What animals do we know?"

I say, "Cat. And dogs and pigeons and squirrels."

"That's dull. I want to get some animal no one else knows about."

"Hey, how about a praying mantis? I saw one once in Gramercy Park."

Ben doesn't even know what it is, so I tell him about this one I saw. For an insect, it looks almost like a dragon, about four or five inches long and pale green. When it flies, it looks like a baby helicopter in the sky. We go into Gramercy Park to see if we can find another, but we can't.

Ben says, "Let's go up to the Bronx Zoo Saturday and see what we can find."

"Stupid, they don't mean you to do lions and tigers. They're not native."

"Stupid, yourself. They got other animals that are. Besides, there's lots of woods and ponds. I might find something."

Well, it's as good an idea for Saturday as any, so I say O.K. On account of both being pretty broke, we take lunch along in my old school lunchbox. Also six subway tokens—two extras for emergencies. Even I would be against walking home from the Bronx.

Of course there are plenty of native New York City animals in the zoo—raccoons and woodchucks and moles and lots of birds—and I figure we better start home not too late to get out the encyclopedias for species and life cycles. Ben still wants to catch something wild and wonderful. Like lots of city kids who haven't been in the country much, he's crazy about nature.

We head back to the subway, walking through the woods so he can hunt. We go down alongside the pond and kick up rocks and dead trees to see if anything is under them.

It pays off. All of a sudden we see a tiny red tail

disappearing under a rotten log. I push the log again and Ben grabs. It's a tiny lizard, not more than two or three inches long and brick red all over. Ben cups it in both hands, and its throat pulses in and out, but it doesn't really try to get away.

"Hey, I love this one!" Ben cries. "I'm going to take him home and keep him for a pet, as well as do a report on him. You can't keep cats and dogs in Peter Cooper, but there's nothing in the rules about lizards."

"How are you going to get him home?"

"Dump the lunch. I mean—we'll eat it, but I can stab a hole in the top of the box, and keep Redskin in it. Come on, hurry! He's getting tired in my hand I think!"

Ben is one of those guys who is very placid most of the time, but he gets excitable all of a sudden when he runs into something brand-new to him, and I guess he never caught an animal to keep before. Some people's parents are very stuffy about it.

I dump the lunch out, and he puts the lizard in and selects some particular leaves and bits of dead log to put in with him to make him feel at home. Without even asking me, he takes out his knife and makes holes in the top of my lunchbox. I sit down and open up a sandwich, but Ben is still dancing around.

"What do you suppose he is? He might be something very rare! How'm I going to find out? You think we ought to go back and ask one of the zoo men?"

"Umm, nah," I say, chewing. "Probably find him in the encyclopedia."

Ben squats on a log, and the log rolls. As he falls over backward I see two more lizards scuttle away. I grab one. "Hey, look! I got another. This one's bigger and browner."

Ben is up and dancing again. "Oh, boy, oh, boy! Now I got two! Now they'll be happy! Maybe they'll have babies, huh?"

He overlooks the fact that *I* caught this one. Oh, well, I don't want a lizard, anyway. Cat'd probably eat it.

Ben takes it from me and slips it in the lunchbox. "I'm going to call this one Big Brownie."

Finally he calms down enough to eat lunch, taking peeks at his catch between mouthfuls. As soon as he's finished eating, he starts hustling to get home so he can make a house for them. He really acts like a kid.

We get on the subway. It's above ground—elevated—up here in the Bronx. After a while I see Yankee Stadium off to one side, which is funny because I don't remember seeing it when we were coming up. Pretty soon the train goes underground. I remember then.

Coming up, we changed trains once. Ben has his eye glued to the edge of the lunchbox and he's talking to Redskin, so I figure there's no use consulting him. I'll just wait and see where this train seems to come out. It's got to go downtown. We go past something called Lenox Avenue, which I think is in Harlem, then Ninety-sixth Street, and then we're at Columbus Circle.

"Hey, Ben, we're on the West Side subway," I say.

"Yeah?" He takes a bored look out the window.

"We can just walk across town from Fourteenth Street."

"With you I always end up walking. Hey, what about those extra tokens?"

"Aw, it's only a few blocks. Let's walk."

Ben grunts, and he goes along with me. As we get near Union Square, there seem to be an awful lot of people around. In fact they're jamming the sidewalk and we can hardly move. Ben frowns at them and says, "Hey, what goes?"

I ask a man, and he says, "Where you been, sonny? Don'tcha know there's a parade for General Sparks?"

I remember reading about it now, so I poke Ben. "Hey, push along! We can see Sparks go by."

"Quit pushing and don't try to be funny."

"Stupid, he's a general. Test pilot, war hero, and stuff. Come on, push."

"QUIT PUSHING! I got to watch out for these lizards!"

So I go first and edge us through the crowd to the middle of the block, where there aren't so many people, and we can get up next to the police barrier. Cops on horseback are going back and forth, keeping the street clear. No sign of any parade coming yet, but people are throwing rolls of paper tape and handfuls of confetti out of upper-story windows. The wind catches the paper tape and carries it up and around in all kinds of fantastic snakes. Little kids keep scuttling under the barrier to grab handfuls of ticker tape that blow to the ground. Ben keeps one eye on the street and one on Redskin and Brownie.

"How soon you think they're coming?" he asks fretfully.

People have packed in behind us, and we couldn't leave now if we wanted to. Pretty soon we can see a helicopter flying low just a little ways downtown, and people all start yelling, "That's where they are! They're coming!"

Suddenly a bunch of motorcycle cops zoom past, and then a cop backing up a police car at about thirty miles an hour, which is a very surprising-looking thing. Before I've hardly got my eyes off that, the open

cars come by. This guy Sparks is sitting up on the back
of the car, waving with both hands. By the time I see
him, he's almost past. Nice-looking, though. Everyone
yells like crazy and throws any kind of paper they've
got. Two little nuts beside us have a box of Wheaties,
so they're busy throwing Breakfast of Champions. As
soon as the motorcade is past, people push through the
barriers and run in the street.

Ben hunches over to protect his precious animals
and yells, "Come on! Let's get out of this!"

We go into my house first because I'm pretty sure
we've got a wooden box. We find it and take it down
to my room, and Ben gets extra leaves and grass and
turns the lizards into it. He's sure they need lots of
fresh air and exercise. Redskin scoots out of sight into
a corner right away. Big Brownie sits by a leaf and
looks around.

"Let's go look up what they are," I say.

The smallest lizard they show in the encyclopedia is
about six inches long, and it says lizards are reptiles
and have scales and claws and should not be confused
with salamanders, which are amphibians and have
thin moist skin and no claws. So we look up salamanders.

This is it, all right. The first picture on the page
looks just like Redskin, and it says he's a Red Eft. The

Latin name for his species is *Triturus viridescens,* or in English just a common newt.

"Hey, talk about life cycles, listen to this," says Ben, reading. " 'It hatches from an egg in the water and stays there during its first summer as a dull-green larva. Then its skin becomes a bright orange, it absorbs its gills, develops lungs and legs, and crawls out to live for about three years in the woods. When fully mature, its back turns dull again, and it returns to the water to breed.' "

Ben drops the book. "Brownie must be getting ready to breed! What'd I tell you? We got to put him near water!" He rushes down to my room.

We come to the door and stop short. There's Cat, poised on the edge of the box.

I grab, but no kid is as fast as a cat. Hearing me coming, he makes his grab for the salamander. Then he's out of the box and away, with Big Brownie's tail hanging out of his mouth. He goes under the bed.

Ben screams, "Get him! Kill him! He's got my Brownie!" He's in a frenzy, and I don't blame him. It does make you mad to see your pet get hurt. I run for a broom to try to poke Cat out, but it isn't any use. Meanwhile, Ben finds Redskin safe in the box, and he scoops him back into the lunchbox.

Finally, we move the bed, and there is Cat poking daintily with his paw at Brownie. The salamander is dead. Ben grabs the broom and bashes Cat. Cat hisses and skids down the hall. "That rotten cat! I wish I could kill him! What'd you ever have him for?"

I tell Ben I'm sorry, and I get him a little box so he can bury Brownie. You can't really blame Cat too much—that's just the way a cat is made, to chase anything that wiggles and runs. Ben calms down after a while, and we go back to the encyclopedia to finish looking up about the Red Eft.

"I don't think Brownie was really ready to lay eggs, or he would have been in the pond already," I say. "Tell you what. We could go back some day with a jar and try to catch one in the water."

That cheers Ben up some. He finishes taking notes for his report and tracing a picture, and then he goes home with Redskin in the lunchbox. I pull out the volume for C.

Cat. Family, *Felidae*, including lions and tigers. Species, *Felis domesticus*. I start taking notes: " 'The first civilized people to keep cats were the Egyptians, thirteen centuries before Christ. . . . Fifty million years earlier the ancestor of the cat family roamed the earth, and he is the ancestor of all present-day carnivores. The Oligocene cats, thirty million years ago, were already highly specialized, and the habits and physical characteristics of cats have been fixed since then. This may explain why house cats remain the most independent of pets, with many of the instincts of their wild ancestors.' "

I call Ben up to read him this, and he says, "You and your lousy carnivore! *My* salamander is an amphibian, and amphibians are the ancestors of *all* animals on earth, even you and your Cat, you sons of toads!"

ADAM BOOKOUT

by Louisa R. Shotwell

When Adam was eleven, his parents were killed in a plane crash, and Adam had to leave their ranch to live with his great-aunts in a small Oklahoma town. He didn't like this very much and hoped a visit with his father's cousins in Brooklyn would help: new scenes, new school, new friends. . . .

It was Wednesday afternoon, Adam's third day in school.

Saul pushed his thick-lensed, horn-rimmed glasses

up to the top of his nose where they belonged. They always kept slipping and sliding.

"See you," said Saul. "*Ankylosaurus*."

"*Triceratops*," said Adam.

The green traffic light turned to yellow.

Adam watched Saul, pint-sized and stocky, stride off across the street at a rolling pace, shoulders swaying, stubby-toed shoes pointing outward at every step. Saul had to go take his Hebrew lesson, and he was late.

For three days now Adam had known Saul, and if he should meet him on a South Sea island or in Timbuctoo, wearing no glasses and with every tight blond curl shaved off his head, he would recognize that walk.

Even without the password, Adam would know Saul, anywhere in this world or outer space.

Saul had a headlong approach to friendship that made Adam uneasy, at first. Indeed, it struck Adam that Saul was almost as much of a problem as Hank Wilmot, only in the opposite way. Hank was not interested in Adam at all, where he came from or anything about him. Saul was entirely too interested.

The first thing Monday morning he launched a barrage of questions. Beecy's warning echoed in Adam's head: *Questions mean trouble.* The sharp recollection of Auntie Vann's pecking at him set his teeth on edge, and his early answers to Saul's catechism were wary.

It did not take too long, though, to realize that Saul was a different kettle of fish from Auntie Vann. Just what kind of fish was uncertain, but he was no more like Auntie Vann than he was like Hank Wilmot. In the course of that first day Adam came to see that Saul made a business of acquiring facts. He was curious, he knew his way around school, he enjoyed telling you off, and the more you talked back to him the better he liked you.

The minute Adam walked into 6-3 on Monday morning, the teacher, a man named Mr. North, told him he would have to sit at a table in the back of the room because the regular desks were all filled. Adam was hardly in his seat when the boy beside him began.

"Saul is the name. S-a-u-l K-a-t-z—pronounced *cats*. Saul Katz. And yours?"

"Adam."

"Adam, like in the Garden of Eden?"

"That's it."

"Adam what?"

"Bookout."

"How do you spell it?"

"How does it sound?"

"B-o-o-k-o-u-t?"

"Right."

"Bookout. Rhymes with cookout. Adam Bookout. I've got it. Where'd you go to school before?"

"Oklahoma."

"Oklahoma! No kidding! Oil wells? Tepees? Covered wagons?"

"Cattle." Adam thawed slightly.

"Oh, a cowboy. You ride in here on horseback?"

"I flew."

"Who with?"

"Myself."

"Nobody else?"

"Nobody else. Except for Beecy."

"Who's Beecy?"

"A girl I met on the way."

Saul whistled.

"You needn't whistle. She only helped me buy my plane ticket. She got off at St. Louis. After that I slept."

"Where you living?"

"With my cousins."

"Where's that?"

"Van Hooten Terrace."

"How do you like it?"

"It's O.K. It's good."

"Where'd you get the necktie?"

"It's a hand-me-down."

"Who from?"

"My cousin Johnnie Bookout."

"You wear it as if it belonged on you. Wish I could

do that. All it takes for me to look like a fish out of water is a necktie. You just may be able to get away with that necktie in 6-3, seeing it's a little frayed."

Mr. North yelled at them to be quiet, and Saul lowered his voice.

"This truck he's handing out now is Social Studies. He's finishing up on our Latin American neighbors, but you wait till after lunch. No, this is Monday. You'll have to wait till tomorrow afternoon. We get a different teacher then; his name is Mr. Appleby and he's beginning us on dinosaurs. You had those yet in Oklahoma?"

"Not yet."

All day long Saul kept showing Adam the ropes.

By Tuesday afternoon, when Mr. Appleby appeared, Adam had almost forgotten he was a newcomer. He knew the ropes, he had a friend named Saul Katz, and he was well on the way to being an old-timer in 6-3.

Mr. Appleby made a short speech on dinosaurs.

Saul, sharing his textbook with Adam, pounced on *ankylosaurus*.

"Passwords are useful," he said. "Which one will you take?"

"What for?" asked Adam.

"For passwords, the way I said, dopey. Can't you pay attention?"

"What good are passwords?"

"To identify your friends in the dark, stupid. In a blackout, or in a holdup, or any such time. You never know when you may need to use it. I'll be this twenty-foot walking fortress with the spiky shell on top." He pointed to the picture of *ankylosaurus*. "That's my name. Which one do you want?"

Adam eyed the caption under the picture.

"Your old twenty-foot walking fortress is nothing but a harmless vegetarian," he said. "Eats nothing but vegetables. It says so, right there in print. Why do you want to be a harmless vegetarian?"

"I am, anyway, sort of," said Saul. "I'm harmless. Hey! Here's what you can be. Look!" He pointed to *tyrannosaurus*. " 'The largest, fiercest meat-eater that ever lived, with teeth six inches long and a mouth as big as a power shovel.' How about that?"

"Not me," said Adam. "I'll be this little guy here with three horns sticking out of his face. I only weigh ten tons."

The boys rocked with mirth, clutching their stomachs to keep from bursting. Adam had not laughed so hard since Auntie Meg told her story about the pumpkin.

Mr. Appleby came over to see what the joke was, but they didn't tell. They did ask him how to pronounce their two tongue twisters, though, repeating after him *ankylosaurus* and *triceratops* until he said they had them right.

"How about *tyrannosaurus?*" asked Mr. Appleby. "And *diplodocus?* Hadn't you better learn to pronounce those, too?"

"Two of them are enough for today," said Saul. "That's all our heads will hold." Again, he and Adam hung on to their stomachs to check their snorts.

Mr. Appleby was a good-natured teacher and didn't care if you thought something was funny. He didn't even care if you talked out loud while you were supposed to be studying. If you kept it low, that is, then he didn't care.

"He's the science specialist. Nothing bothers him," Saul said. "He comes to 6-3 Friday afternoons, too, so Mr. North can take a breather. He needs it. He's a nervous type."

When Mr. North was in charge, everybody talked a lot louder than when Mr. Appleby was there, and Mr. North did care, very much. He kept yelling and yelling at them to stop. The buzz would slacken for a minute, and then it would zoom out louder than ever.

Magdalena cared, too, about the talking and all the noise, even the amount Mr. Appleby allowed. It bothered her, you could see that. Magdalena was the third person at their table, a skinny girl with long black braids and a tiny gold ring which went through each ear lobe, straight through. She tossed her braids, picked up her book, and turned her chair around to face the wall. With her book open on her lap and her elbows resting on it, she put a finger in each ear.

"Don't mind her," said Saul. "She can't help it. She's stuck-up because pretty soon they're putting her into the I.G.C. class."

"What's I.G.C.?" asked Adam.

"Intellectually Gifted Child. Brother, do you have a lot to learn!"

Wednesday afternoon, after Saul's figure had merged with the street-crossing crowd and vanished, Adam sauntered along Indiana Avenue toward Van Hooten Terrace, Johnnie Bookout's castoff schoolbag hanging from his shoulder.

Circling an untidy heap of vegetable crates in front of a supermarket, he walked around a man selling carnations and paused briefly to admire the way different-sized nails and nuts and bolts were set out in little open boxes on a beat-up wooden platform on wheels. This was nice. The clerk could roll the platform out when he opened the store, and roll it back in when closing time came or when it rained.

The sun glinted on the red-white-and-blue striped

pole spinning dizzily in a glass case outside a barber shop.

Before the next store front he came to a dead stop.

He'd seen it first on his way home from school on Monday. The next day, and now again on Wednesday, he stood with eyes glued to the glass, watching a puppy frolicking on a bed of shredded newspapers. A real puppy, silky-black, lively as a monkey, and twice as cute.

Adam tapped softly on the glass. The puppy cocked his head on one side and batted his eyes, as if to say, "Now where in the world have I see you before?"

Adam had not had a dog in years, not since Maxie, their white Collie, took to killing chickens, and they had to give him away. Lately, with plenty of horses around, Adam had not given much thought to dogs. But now . . .

After a while the puppy in the window turned around three times and snuggled down into the shredded newspapers to take a nap.

Reluctantly, Adam moved on.

The idea hit him as he turned the corner into Van Hooten Terrace. He was not positive, but it had the feeling of another brain storm.

He could buy himself a dog.

Why not?

There were reasons why not, mainly that his money supply was dwindling. The taxi ride from the airport and Mr. Gutowski's tip had cut into it very deep. Sunday night Cousin Kate had given him five days' lunch money and a dollar extra for cokes and candy bars and other emergencies through the week. The extra dollar had thirty cents left to it, and that would be gone by Saturday.

Perhaps when the Oklahoma money matters stopped being somewhat unclear, Mr. H. O. Miller would let him have enough to buy a dog. Or he could go to work after school and earn it. There must be plenty of jobs in a city this big, paper routes and shining shoes and such things.

He had no idea how much a dog would cost.

Well, he could find out, couldn't he? It wouldn't cost anything to ask.

By this time, without noticing he'd moved a foot since the brain storm hit, he stood on the steps of the Bookout apartment house. Robert saw him coming and opened the street door.

"Good afternoon, Adam," he said. "You look like the cat that swallowed the canary. What's new?"

"Nothing," said Adam. "I mean, everything."

Riding up alone in the elevator, he made up his mind. He would go into that store tomorrow after school and find out how much it would cost to buy a dog.

Next morning, in the middle of Language Arts, a new boy showed up in grade 6-3.

Everybody kept quiet to watch if Mr. North would blow his top on account of getting another extra pupil when he didn't have room for what he already had.

Mr. North did not blow his top, but it was easy to see he'd have liked to.

The new boy was tall. He walked in gently on the balls of his feet, looking bashful. He looked as if he wished he were somewhere else, anywhere at all excepting in grade 6-3.

Mr. North had him take the very last chair at the table in the back of the room, alongside of Adam and Saul and Magdalena.

Just the way he'd done with Adam, Saul went to firing questions at the newcomer, not wasting a minute.

The new boy's name was Willie Weggfall.

He had come in from Alabama four days ago.

No, he did not fly in on an airplane.

No, he did not come by bus, or by train, either, and no, he did not hitchhike. Willie Weggfall had ridden up from Alabama in an automobile with his uncle. No, his uncle did not own the automobile.

"Did he rent it?"

Willie bit his lip. Adam knew how he felt.

"He borrowed it," said Willie.

"Who from?"

"From a friend on the top floor, if it makes any difference to you."

"Relax. I didn't say he stole it. The top floor of what?"

"The top floor of the house where my folks in Brooklyn live, my uncle and aunt and their kids. Are you from the F.B.I.?"

"They wouldn't have me. I'm not old enough. I do like to get a line on people, though, if they're interesting. You're interesting, walking in here looking as if it was a jail. No offense. How many kids?"

"Don't let Saul get your goat," said Adam. "He put me through the third degree, too, my first day here. He's nosy, but he's harmless. You may as well tell him. He won't stop till you do."

"How many kids?" asked Saul, again.

"See what I mean?" said Adam.

Willie wriggled in his chair, cast an eye at Saul and then at Adam, and finally laughed.

"Two kids, a boy name of Jonathan, and a girl, Melinda. He's ten and she's seven, almost eight. And their grandmother, she lives there too. I don't know how old she is. So what else do you want to know?"

"Several things." Saul proceeded with his inquisition.

No, Willie never had been north before, and yes, his regular folks, his mother and father and the rest, still lived in Minter County, Alabama.

How were things in Minter County, Alabama?

Quick as lightning Willie came back with, "How are things in Brooklyn?" He was holding up his end all right with Saul.

"Middling. Why'd you come here?"

"To see if I liked it."

"You aim to stay? Live here with your uncle and his family?"

"Maybe. If I feel like it."

"Where do they live?"

"Van Hooten Terrace."

"Hey! That's where Adam lives. That's Adam with the necktie, the one sizes me up nosy but harmless, he lives in Van Hooten Terrace, too."

Mr. North yelled at them to be quiet.

He was busy explaining about Sharing Our Emotions, and if they did not listen, he told the class, they would not know how to do it.

What it meant was, everybody was supposed to read a book and come to class prepared to tell whether it made them laugh or cry or get mad or scared, or what, and why.

Hands waved in the air.

Nearly everyone in 6-3 had a question to ask.

Did it have to be a book from the School Library?

Could it be a book from the Public Library, or from home?

Could it be a book your mother bought at the supermarket?

Would science fiction count?

How about a book on the Battle of Gettysburg? Or baseball? Or choosing your vocation?

Nothing factual, said Mr. North, and no how-to books, not this time. Stories.

If it was a story about baseball or your vocation, would it do? Or a story on a battle? Any old battle?

Would it be all right if it was a true story about a dog?

How could you tell ahead of time if you were going to like it, so reading it would not be a waste of your valuable energy? This one came from Saul.

And so on.

All important things to know.

Under the cover of the questions, Adam hissed at Willie Weggfall:

"*Psst!* What number does your uncle live at on Van Hooten Terrace?"

"Number Eleven," Willie whispered.

Adam made a circle with his thumb and forefinger and gave him the eye, and Willie made a circle in return.

After school, Willie hung back and almost lost himself in the mob. Saul looked over his shoulder till he spotted him. "What's the matter? Aren't you coming, Willie? Don't you want to go home?"

"I guess," said Willie.

"All right, quit acting as if you're too proud to walk with your friends."

"I'm not all that proud," said Willie.

"Then step on it, snail."

Saul Katz and Willie Weggfall, two good kids.

It was lucky for Adam, after all, that Mr. North's room was short on regular desks.

"Wow!" said Adam.

He said it twice.

The first time was in the pet store when the man told him the price of the silky black puppy in the window.

Seventy-five dollars.

Seventy-five dollars! Wow!

It would take a year to earn that much after school.

"We have other dogs," said the man. "The others

are more expensive, of course. The black cocker you saw in the window is a bargain, because he's under-sized. The standard poodles start at a hundred and twenty-five, and the dachshunds . . ."

"Never mind." Adam was totally uninterested. Even if he could have bought one of those other dogs for seventy-five cents, or for nothing, he had eyes for none except the silky-black puppy.

Beside him, Willie Weggfall spoke into his ear.

"Let's get out of this place."

That made sense.

On the sidewalk, as the door swung shut behind them, Adam said it again.

"Wow!"

This time the *wow* meant he was glad for a whiff of fresh air.

"What a stink! Like a circus, only fifty times worse. It's a shame. Wouldn't you think that man could fix his place, scrub it or something, so that poor little black puppy in the window wouldn't have to breathe such awful air?"

"Come along," said Willie. "I want to show you something."

"What?"

"You'll see. Get moving."

Willie lengthened his stride. He had very long legs. Adam skipped to catch up.

"Where is it?" he asked.

"At my house. My uncle's house."

Walking fast, they soon reached the corner of Van Hooten Terrace. Willie's house, standing at the opposite end of the block from the Bookout apartment building, was shingled dark gray, and very wide. It was not a house you would expect to find in a city, or anywhere else, actually, not any place where Adam ever had been. A row of square white pillars trimmed in red went straight to the roof, and behind them were five separate porches with railings, and five front doors.

Willie stopped before the third front door, number eleven.

"Wait here," he said. "I'll be right back." He disappeared inside.

There was a patch of yard in front of each porch. Three of the yards were scrubby looking, ash cans lying on their sides, and a derelict refrigerator in one yard. The Weggfalls' yard looked tidy. Their ash can stood straight up and was covered tight. A bunch of little kids were playing on the porch just beyond, and the porch on the near side had a white iron cemetery bench on it. For sitting? It did not look comfortable, and it was chained to the railing.

The Weggfalls' door opened and Willie reappeared . . . with a dog!

Willie had him on a leash.

Bright brown hair, white spot over one eye, tail curled into a perfect letter O.

The dog scooted straight for Adam, pulling Willie along after, and began jumping up and licking Adam's face and hands.

"Golly!" said Adam. "He's terrific! Whose is he?"

"She," said Willie. "He's a she, and she's mine. All mine." He sat down on the step. The dog jumped into his lap.

"Where'd you get him? Her?"

"I had her in Alabama. She rode up along with me in the car. She's a good traveler." Willie slid over to make room for Adam on the step.

"What's her name?"

"Honey. On account of her color, see? She's the color of red clover honey, aren't you, Honey?" He fondled her under the chin. Honey shut her eyes and lay quiet, telling him to keep on doing that.

Adam stroked her with one finger. Her hair was soft, not too long, and curled a little on the ends.

"Is she a cocker?"

"I'm not so sure she's any one particular kind. My daddy says she's most likely a mutt and they can be the very best."

"It's a neat harness she's wearing." The harness was green, with silver knobs decorating it all along. The leash was green, too, and had those same silver knobs to match the harness.

"It's new. We just bought it, Monday. It's better than a collar. It costs more but there's less strain on her neck and more style. The leash is new, too. Gran Dee bought them for her. I started to pay, I have this five dollar bill my daddy gave me and a fifty cent piece from my mother, but Gran Dee said no, she wanted to give Honey a present so she would know she's welcome in Brooklyn."

"Who's Gran Dee?"

"She's grandmother to my uncle's kids. Everybody calls her Gran Dee. She's O.K. Honey can't get used to being on a leash, not yet. She ran wild in Alabama."

"Did your folks have to pay seventy-five dollars to get her for you?"

"What do you think? Not much, they didn't. My folks wouldn't know what seventy-five dollars looks like. Neither would I."

"Then how did you get her? Somebody give her to you?"

"No, not that, either. She just showed up at our place one sundown, all scraggly with mud and nettles, and her tail adroop. She had a deep cut behind her ears, jagged as if somebody'd lashed her with a whip wound in barbed wire. My mother set out a pie tin of chitterlings in the yard and she sniffed and wouldn't eat. Louanne, she's my sister, she fixed her some good cold well water in a saucer, but she wouldn't even drink. My daddy tried examining the bad place on her neck and she snapped at him. Look, you can still find the scar where the new hair can't quite cover it. See how crooked it is?"

"Mean! How mean can a person get! Then what? After she snapped at your father?"

"My daddy said we'd best leave her be till she got to trust us. He said if we let the chitterlings sit, and the water, and go away, she might eat or drink. So we went in the house. I stood inside the screen door, watching and watching. She slunk out toward the road but kept looking back, as if she couldn't make up her mind should she go or come. By and by she turned and stepped along slow toward the water. She lapped a couple of laps and laid herself down like fixing to rest a spell. I stole outside and stretched myself on the ground close to the stoop, not too near where she was. I shut my eyes. In a while, it seemed an awful long while, I felt something cold and wet on my face. There she was, licking me. So then I petted her some and talked to her real soft, and separated out a few of the nettles from her hair and I whistled to Louanne to bring some warm water and a rag. I sat up and cleaned the cut place on her neck. Louanne took the chitterlings away and filled the pie tin with white meat of chicken and some collards left from supper. She still would not eat off the pie tin, but when I fed her out of my hand, one small piece after another, why, then, she ate. So that's how she's my dog. She stayed on with us right along until her neck healed. None of our neighbors in the quarters ever had seen her before and nobody came asking, so we kept her. That's how come she's mine."

"I wish I had a dog. A good dog like Honey."

"They can't all cost seventy-five dollars. You find one cheaper, your folks might buy her for you."

"It's not likely. They aren't that well acquainted with me."

"Aren't they your real folks?"

"They're my real cousins. I've only been with them about a week. They're nice, but not like it's your regular parents. They have four children of their own, besides me. They're all off at boarding school or college, all except Sandy. He's a Marine in California."

"I'd like to be a Marine in California, or some place. I will, too, some day. Where'd you live before?"

"Oklahoma, with my aunties. I didn't like it much at their house. Auntie Meg was all right but Auntie Vann kept pestering me and I remembered about these cousins in Brooklyn. I'd never seen them but I came anyhow. I'm not going back, either, not for quite a while. I certainly would like to have a dog. Do you think you'll stay here? Till you're ready to go be a Marine, I mean?"

"I don't know. It depends, if I get along."

"Didn't you get along in Alabama?" It hit Adam suddenly that he was being as nosy as Saul, but he had to hear about this.

Willie acted wound up.

"I get mad pretty easy. You saw that this morning when Saul asked me all those questions. We had a little trouble down home, folks stirred up to register for voting, demonstration marches and like that. You must have heard how it's been. My folks didn't set store by any of it but I did, these civil rights really burn me up, and I went fetching water for the marchers and carrying messages. I marched some, too. They mostly tried to keep children out of the line but I was so tall, they didn't notice. Uncle Oscar saw about it on television and . . ."

"You? He saw you on television?"

"Not me. I don't mean he saw about me but he saw it was going on in our county. When they brought out the tear gas, he could see worse around the corner so he took himself five days annual leave from the post office and borrowed the car off Melinda's friend Barbie

Anne's father on the top floor and drove down to see how we were making out and hadn't we better move north. My folks were scared, all right, but they wouldn't leave home."

"Why not?"

"They were scared to stay and they were scareder to move north, so they stayed."

"Why were they scared to move north?"

"My daddy didn't know how he'd make out for work. He has a steady job in the sawmill down home, as steady as a job can be in a sawmill and he wants to hang on to it. That's why he won't hold with registering to vote or marching or boycotting stores or anything that could make him get fired. What he said was, a man ought to live where he fits. He knew he fit in Minter County, Alabama, born and raised there, and he couldn't see himself lasting through one winter up north. All that snow and ice, he wouldn't feel at home."

"How did he happen to let you come?"

"I expect he was afraid I'd bring trouble if I hung around home much longer. He didn't say so, though. All he told me was, I might not be old enough to learn where I fit but I was sure tall enough. I could go hunting the right place for me if I felt like it. He didn't know but I ought to give Brooklyn a shot. It'd be like Honey trying us out, and finding she belonged to me. I might find I belonged in Brooklyn. And he told me . . ."

Willie leaned down and examined Honey's scar.

"He told you what?"

"Nothing much."

"Nothing much what?"

"He only told me . . . wherever I go, up north or anywhere, I mustn't look to find heaven on earth. Home is what you make it where you are, he said, and I'd need to watch my step. Hang on to my temper, I guess he meant."

"What did your mother say?"

"She said wherever my daddy was, did he go or did he stay, she'd go or stay according. Any time the Lord went looking for her, she said, if He would only locate my daddy, that's where she'd be, too, through thick or thin. About me, she said she wouldn't worry herself, knowing I'd have Honey along for company. Uncle Oscar said he hadn't figured on a dog but he didn't know why not and did I have a few rabbits or a possum would want to come? The back seat was empty. I said no, only Honey. So here we are, me and my dog."

He stood up, tumbling Honey to the ground. "Come on. Honey needs exercise. She needs to practice with her leash."

They strolled along the block toward Adam's corner.

At first Honey snapped and bit at the leash, and then all at once she gave up and trotted along as easy as a horse.

When they came to the door of Number One, Adam said:

"Here's my place. Come on in. We can show Honey to Cousin Kate. She'll like her. Come along. Will you?"

"I don't know if I should," said Willie.

"Oh, come on."

Robert opened the door. "Bless my soul, Adam Bookout. What's this I see? Not a *dog!*"

"Her name is Honey," said Adam. "She's Willie's. Isn't she terrific? This is Willie Weggfall. We're taking Honey up to show her to Cousin Kate. Is she home?"

"She's home," said Robert, looking sober. "But Honey can't come in."

"Honey can't come in! Why ever not?" Adam looked hard at Robert to see if he could be teasing but there was no sign. "She's only going to visit."

"Not even to visit," said Robert, still sober. "I am sorry, kids, really I am, but rules are rules, and the management is very strict about dogs. Very strict indeed."

"Well!" said Adam. "How do you like that!"

"I ought to've had more sense," said Willie. "My father warned me."

"The management must be crazy," said Adam.

Robert bristled. "That's no way to talk, Adam Bookout. The management is not crazy. They simply have an ironclad rule about dogs, cats, and monkeys. Birds and goldfish are allowed and so are boys, as long as they behave. You leave your dog at home, Willie Weggfall, you come in with Adam any time you please. Is that plain?"

"I can?" asked Willie.

"You heard me," said Robert.

"I still say it's crazy," said Adam.

"Pay it no mind," said Willie. "I need to walk Honey some more, anyhow. I'll take her round the square. See you tomorrow, Adam."

"See you," said Adam, waving a hand.

He stood in the doorway, looking, until Willie and Honey turned the corner.

BIOGRAPHICAL NOTES

NAN HAYDEN AGLE grew up in Catonsville, Maryland, and lives today in a small house in the woods just outside Baltimore. She taught art for a number of years at Friends School in Baltimore and was also associated with the Baltimore Museum of Art. Among Mrs. Agle's pupils were several girls who later came to mind when she was creating the character of Margaret Gage, heroine of *Maple Street*. Mrs. Agle has written a number of other books on her own and was co-author of the popular Three Boys series of stories.

ROSE BLUE, a native New Yorker, teaches pre-kindergarten in the Bedford-Stuyvesant section of Brooklyn. She received her B.A. from Brooklyn College and has done graduate work at Bank Street College of Education. In addition to *A Quiet Place*, Miss Blue, long a free-lance writer and lyricist, has a number of stories and records to her credit.

NELLIE BURCHARDT was born in Philadelphia, Pennsylvania. She received her B.A. from Queens College, Flushing, New York, and her M.A. from Yale University. Mrs. Burchardt did graduate study in library science at Columbia University while a trainee at the New York City Public Library. *Reggie's No-Good Bird* was the second of her books for children, *Project Cat* being the first.

JOHN DURHAM, who holds an M.A. in English from the State University of Iowa and a Ph.D. from Occidental College in Los Angeles, has been a high school teacher and a college professor. He was a resident writer on a Los Angeles School District project to produce high-interest, easy-reading textbooks designed to meet the needs of disadvantaged students. The idea for *Me and Arch and the Pest* grew out of this work. Dr. Durham is also the author of *Queen of Diamonds, Take the Short Way Home*, and several short stories for young readers.

DALE FIFE lives in San Mateo, California, where she spends a good deal of her time writing. *Who's in Charge of Lincoln* is but one of her many books, including two others about her popular hero Abraham Lincoln. For *Walk a Narrow Bridge* she won the 1967 Juvenile Award presented by the Martha Kinney Cooper Ohioana Library Association. Miss Fife also writes books for adults.

PAULA FOX, a teacher at Ethical Culture School in New York City and mother of two sons, could very well have drawn from her own environment for *Maurice's Room*. At the time the book appeared, one son's room featured a dog, a parrot, a chameleon, a tank of tropical fish—and a striking collection of just plain junk. Mrs. Fox has also worked on newspapers here and abroad and has had television plays produced on "Naked City."

ELEANOR HULL was born in Denver, Colorado. She has an A.A. from the Colorado Woman's College, a B.A. from the University of Redlands, and a B.F.A. from the University of Denver. *A Trainful of Strangers* is one of many books for children written by Mrs. Hull since 1949. She has lived in Hartsdale, New York, for a number of years.

NORMA KEATING, author of *Mr. Chu*, lives in Freehold, New Jersey, and has had two collections of her poetry published, *Songs of a Salamander* and *Giants and Dwarfs*. She has written for the New Reading Material Program, sponsored by the New York Board of Education, and has been a newspaper and magazine columnist.

PEGGY MANN, author of *The Street of the Flower Boxes*, was born in New York City. She received a B.A. from the University of Wisconsin and did graduate study at Columbia University, the New School for Social Research, and the University of Birmingham, England. Miss Mann has also written books for adults and TV and radio scripts and has been a contributor to numerous magazines and newspapers.

EMILY NEVILLE was born in Manchester, Connecticut, the youngest of seven children and cousin to so many that the family hired a teacher and set up its own school. Later she attended the Oxford School in West Hartford, Connecticut. A graduate of Bryn Mawr College, where she majored in economics, Mrs. Neville had thought of a career in research but "happened into a job as a copy girl on the *New York News*, thence to the *New York Mirror*." She and her husband and five children did live in the Gramercy Park area of New York City, setting for *It's Like This, Cat*, but Mrs. Neville now makes her home in St. Louis, Missouri. *It's Like This, Cat* was Mrs. Neville's first novel and won the 1964 Newbery Medal. Two later books written by her have also been awarded honors for outstanding contributions to children's literature.

DORIS ORGEL was born in Vienna, Austria, but left there at the age of nine, spending some time in Yugoslavia and England before coming to the United States in 1940. After graduation from college in 1950, she worked in magazine and book publishing in New York City. Mrs. Orgel now lives in Westport, Connecticut, with her husband and three children, where she divides her time between writing and "an absolute minimum" of household chores. *Next Door to Xanadu* is one of several children's books authored by Mrs. Orgel, whose publications also include two translations and an adaptation of old German fairy tales.

GEORGE SELDEN, a free-lance writer living in New York City, was born in Hartford, Connecticut. He attended the Loomis School in Windsor, Connecticut, and received his B.A. from Yale University. After college he spent a year in Italy on a Fulbright scholarship. He has written numerous books for children since 1956, including *The Cricket in Times Square*, which was a runner-up for the 1961 Newbery Medal. Mr. Selden has also written for TV and film.

LOUISA R. SHOTWELL was born in Chicago and grew up in Skaneateles, New York. She now makes her home in Brooklyn Heights, New York. She received her B.A. from Wellesley College and her M.A. from Stanford University. She has taught English in high school and college and was a staff member of the National Council of Churches Division of Home Missions, where her major assignment was promotional and interpretative writing. In commenting on *Adam Bookout*, Miss Shotwell said she knew she wanted to write a story about a boy who goes to public school in Brooklyn but couldn't seem to focus on him until "one day a Christmas letter arrived from a long lost cousin in Cherokee, Oklahoma —a wheat-harvesting, cattle-raising cousin who flies his own plane—and that was when Adam began to take shape."

MARY STOLZ, the author of more than thirty-five books for young people, including A *Wonderful, Terrible Time*, lives in a colonial house in Stamford, Connecticut, with her husband. She was born in Boston and grew up in New York City, where she attended Birch Wathen School, Columbia University, and the Katharine Gibbs School. Her first jobs included selling books at Macy's and working as a secretary at Teachers College of Columbia University. Besides being an avid reader since childhood—she particularly loves poetry— Mary Stolz has always been a writer. All through school, she put words together—verse, essays, stories, biographies. "I liked anything that could be written about," she says.

YETTA SPEEVACK, author of *The Spider Plant*, was born in Romania and came to America when she was quite young. She studied at Hunter College and Columbia University and in Puerto Rico on a Ford Foundation grant. Miss Speevack has taught in the New York City schools for many years and has lived in New York City.

YOSHIKO UCHIDA is a native Californian, but her life has been rather closely linked to Japan, the native country of her parents. Association with family friends from Japan, observance of Japanese customs in the home, and an avid interest in Japanese folk tales and stories paved the way for Miss Uchida's later study and research for background material for her many writings, among them *The Promised Year*. Miss Uchida has an A.B. from the University of California (Berkeley) and received her M.Ed. from Smith College. She taught second grade at the Japanese Relocation Center in Utah during the Second World War and later taught at Frankford Friends School in Philadelphia. In 1945 she moved to New York City, where her writing career began.

E. B. WHITE grew up in Mount Vernon, New York. After graduation from Cornell University in 1921, he worked in New York for a year then traveled about, trying many sorts of jobs for five or six years before joining the staff of *The New Yorker* magazine and launching a writing career. Mr. White's writing for children was at first purely accidental, starting with *Stuart Little,* a book which developed from a dream that came to him one night on a train and which took some twelve years to materialize, bit by bit. His second book, *Charlotte's Web,* is one of the most delightful and popular of all American children's books of fantasy. In 1970, soon after completing *The Trumpet of the Swan,* he was given the Laura Ingalls Wilder Medal because his books "have over a period of years made a lasting contribution to literature for children." In 1971 Mr. White received the National Book Committee's Medal for Literature for his entire body of work.